"What did you do that for?" April demanded.

The lady packed a hell of a punch, Jimmy thought. He couldn't remember the last time a slight kiss had turned into a full three-course affair. He found himself fighting the urge to do it all over again. "Have you ever felt like you just had to find out something?"

April struggled for her deepest-sounding voice, afraid that anything less would crack. "I generally go to the encyclopedia."

His grin was ever so slightly lopsided. He toyed with a strand of her hair.

"They don't have anything like this in the encyclopedia."

No doubt about it, she thought. Educators and scholars probably hadn't come up with a word to fit what had just happened here....

Dear Reader,

Many people read romance novels for the unforgettable heroes that capture our hearts and stay with us long after the last page is read. But to give all the credit for the success of this genre to these handsome hunks is to underestimate the value of the heart of a romance: the heroine.

"Heroes are fantasy material, but for me, the heroines are much more grounded in real life," says Susan Mallery, bestselling author of this month's *Shelter in a Soldier's Arms*. "For me, the heroine is at the center of the story. I want to write and read about women who are intelligent, funny and determined."

Gina Wilkins's *The Stranger in Room 205* features a beautiful newspaper proprietor who discovers an amnesiac in her backyard and finds herself in an adventure of a lifetime! And don't miss *The M.D. Meets His Match* in Hades, Alaska, where Marie Ferrarella's snowbound heroine unexpectedly finds romance that is sure to heat up the bitter cold....

Peggy Webb delivers an *Invitation to a Wedding;* when the heroine is rescued from marrying the wrong man, could a long-lost friend end up being Mr. Right? Sparks fly in Lisette Belisle's novel when the heroine, raising *Her Sister's Secret Son,* meets a mysterious man who claims to be the boy's father! And in Patricia McLinn's *Almost a Bride,* a rancher desperate to save her ranch enters into a marriage of convenience, but with temptation as her bed partner, life becomes a minefield of desire.

Special Edition is proud to publish novels featuring strong, admirable heroines struggling to balance life, love and family and making dreams come true. Enjoy! And look inside for details about our Silhouette Makes You a Star contest.

Best,

Karen Taylor Richman, Senior Editor

Please address questions and book requests to:
Silhouette Reader Service
U.S.: 3010 Walden Ave., P.O. Box 1325, Buffalo, NY 14269
Canadian: P.O. Box 609, Fort Erie, Ont. L2A 5X3

The M.D. Meets His Match

MARIE FERRARELLA

Silhouette

SPECIAL EDITION™

Published by Silhouette Books

America's Publisher of Contemporary Romance

To Aileen and Adrian Galang,
Happy wedding!
Happy life!
Love,
The Third Photographer

 SILHOUETTE BOOKS

ISBN 0-373-24401-0

THE M.D. MEETS HIS MATCH

Copyright © 2001 by Marie Rydzynski-Ferrarella

Visit Silhouette at www.eHarlequin.com

Printed in U.S.A.

Books by Marie Ferrarella in Miniseries

MARIE FERRARELLA

earned a master's degree in Shakespearean comedy and, perhaps as a result, her writing is distinguished by humor and natural dialogue. This RITA Award-winning author has one goal: to entertain, to make people laugh and feel good. She has written over 100 books for Silhouette, some under the name Marie Nicole. Her romances are beloved by fans worldwide and have been translated into Spanish, Italian, German, Russian, Polish, Japanese and Korean.

SILHOUETTE MAKES YOU A STAR!
Feel like a star with Silhouette.
Look for the exciting details of our new contest inside all of these fabulous Silhouette novels:

Chapter One

With a sigh, April Yearling moved the desk fan closer to her. It was stuffy in the archaic post office, but she couldn't turn the fan on high because it would send the tonnage of envelopes, leaflets and whatnot around her flying off in an unauthorized, frantic dance.

One week back in Hades and she remembered why she'd left.

She mopped her damp forehead with the back of her wrist and instantly regretted it. The area hidden beneath the haphazardly wrapped bandage on her wrist stung, reminding her that there was a consequence for moving too fast, even in a place like Hades.

Biting her lower lip, April continued to sort the mail. She glanced at her watch, swearing that time was altered here in the backstretch of Alaska, moving at a snail's pace that was completely unacceptable to normal human beings.

At least, it was unacceptable to her.

Gran had proudly pointed out that there were people who had moved here from the lower forty-nine. Why a place like Hades, numbering about five hundred on its town roster, would attract anyone to come and settle here was completely beyond April.

Glancing at the scribbled name, she tossed the envelope into its proper pigeonhole.

She moved the fan a tad closer and longed for air-conditioned rooms. It was unseasonably warm for the middle of spring. April couldn't remember a spring ever being so hot and muggy. But this old building wasn't wired for air-conditioning. She supposed she should be happy that it was even wired for electricity, otherwise she'd be relying on candles and the now dormant fireplace in the corner.

A fragment of a memory flashed through her mind. She and her brother and sister gathered around a fireplace, listening to the wind howl outside and the fire crackle as Gran read a ghost story. She remembered waiting to be frightened, but she never was.

Maybe that was her problem, April mused, flipping the last envelope into its cubbyhole. She was too fearless. Nothing frightened her. Except maybe the specter of falling in love.

Small chance of that ever happening, she told herself confidently. She was too smart.

Bending to retrieve more mail out of the sagging pouch Jeb Kellogg had just flown in and dropped off, April smiled. She was a city kid through and through.

It had taken her exactly five minutes in Seattle, her first port of call after graduating high school, to discover that about herself, although she'd secretly thought it for years before her great escape.

There had been this exhilaration that had telegraphed itself through her the moment she'd stepped off the plane and looked around Seattle. She knew then that her soul belonged in a city—the bigger, the better.

April glanced at the next envelope and deposited it where it belonged. Her soul certainly belonged to something bigger than a town comprised of two rows of buildings that faced each other like participants in an old-fashioned square dance.

When she'd left, she'd been positive that nothing would ever bring her back here, here amid the snow and the scenery that went on forever without so much as a soul to disturb it, the loneliness so thick you couldn't cut through it. But of course, her family was here—Gran and Max and June—so there'd been short visits throughout the years. And then she'd received the letter from June saying that Gran, their tiny but invincible tower of strength who had never been ill a day in her life, was sick. Angina, the doctor, Shayne Kerrigan, had said. So she had come back.

It was as simple as that. She owed Gran everything. She and Max and June, they all did. Everything. If Gran hadn't taken them in when their mother had left them in every way but physically, becoming a vacant, broken shell of a woman, April wasn't sure what she would have done. As the oldest by eleven months, she would have had to do something and she had tried.

Tried to care for her brother and sister *and* her mother. But eleven had been a very young age to suddenly become an adult and she hadn't been quite able to manage it.

Until then, she had believed herself up to the challenge. She'd felt she'd grown up rather quickly even before her father had walked out on them and their mother had gone to pieces. Living in a rural town in Alaska was no picnic, no matter what the travel brochures said to the contrary about the frozen state. Alaska, she thought, tossing a fashion magazine onto Edith Plunkett's stack of mail, was an uncompromising mistress who demanded a great deal from everyone who inhabited her terrain.

And right now, she was stuck here. April thrust a postcard into Jean-Luc LeBlanc's pigeonhole. As much as she longed to leave, she felt too worried and too guilty to return to the life she'd placed on hold.

Postmistress. April shook her head. Never in a million years would she have ever seen herself in this position. Gran had even made her take the oath, hand on the Bible and everything. Gran had said it wasn't official otherwise, which meant she couldn't handle the mail when it came through. Gran had taken her position here, both with the government and with the community, very seriously. So April had taken the oath to placate Gran rather than just whisk her away the way she'd wanted to.

April sighed, picking up another envelope. She fervently wished that Max or June had had the time to take over for Gran. But career-wise, neither of them had her flexibility. Max was Hades's sheriff and June was the town's resident mechanic who had more than her share of work to keep up with. That meant she had been elected.

So far, election meant frustration.

It was beyond her why Gran had been so adamant that one of them take over for her here at the post office. It was either that, or have her continue. Gran absolutely refused to turn the job over to an outsider. The position had belonged to someone from Gran's family ever since the first piece of mail had come into Hades some hundred and ten years ago.

As far as April saw it, this was just another rut to leave behind, not something to aspire to.

Certainly not something to take pride in. But Gran took pride in it and Gran was the one who counted, she thought, resigning herself for the umpteenth time and trying desperately to be patient. Patience was not her strong suit. It never had been. She'd always had the sense that there was something else, something better, waiting for her just around the next corner. So she kept turning corners. And anticipating.

April paused to flex her shoulders and straighten her back. "Wanderlust," Gran had called it. She supposed in a way that gave her something in common with her father. The only thing in common. She would never hurt anyone, the way her father had, to get what she wanted. Wayne Yearling had had itchy feet. He'd tried to resist temptation for a while, or so he'd said, but then he'd finally given in and left. Her mother had thought for days that he would return, but April hadn't. Even at eleven, April had known better. She'd known that her father was gone for good.

She'd gotten one postcard from him a few months after he'd left Hades. The only communication she'd ever had from him. One postcard in over thirteen years. The picture had been of Manhattan with its steel-girder skyscrapers making love to the sky as they reached up to forever. She'd fallen in love with the city the second she'd seen the postcard. The inscription on the back had been the typical "Wish you were here" and she wished she was there. Wished it with all her heart.

Gran had slipped the postcard to her, telling her in a hushed voice to not let her mother see it because in her anger and grief, Rose Yearling would have immediately ripped it up. So April kept it like a secret treasure, not even letting Max or June know about it. She'd slipped the postcard beneath her pillow and dreamed dreams of New York City and other places that had never seen a dogsled.

It had taken April seven years to make her dream come true. Her mother was gone by then and there seemed little reason to remain in Alaska. Gran could take care of June, and Max was almost grown. So she had left Hades to make something of herself, to forge a career that suited her and the wanderlust she'd inherited.

She found her answer and her calling in freelance photography and proceeded to make a minor name for herself. That she never remained long in any one particular place was just a pleasant by-product of her career. She went where the stories were and considered herself a citizen of the world rather than as someone belonging to a tiny blip on the map.

Sighing, she ran a hand through the tangle of blond hair that refused to fall into neat waves the way June's always did. Her hair, Gran used to say, was every bit as rebellious as her soul. She supposed that it was. April had always rather liked the description. It made her view her hair as a badge of some kind rather than just a sea of golden corkscrew curls that repeatedly defied styling.

According to one of her acquaintances, she was in style now. Eventually, she mused with an absent smile, everything was.

Digging out another stack of envelopes from inside the mail pouch, the frown that returned to her lips deepened. It was too quiet for her.

Returning to Hades, she'd forgotten how quiet it could be here at times. How quiet and how dark. It was spring now so the endless winter darkness that assaulted the town was six months away, but even so, once the lights went out, there would be nothing but inkiness in the world right outside her window. Nothing like in the city where there were always streetlights and illumination coming in from all sides.

Here, dark was dark, like the bottom of the mine shafts that half the male population of Hades regarded as their prime source of livelihood.

Dark like a soul without love.

She stopped. Where had that come from? In the spring a young man's fancy lightly turns to thoughts of love, she recalled Tennyson's line. Maybe a young man's, but not hers. Love would turn her into someone who was needy. Someone who could be hurt. Like her mother. She'd vowed that was never going to happen to her.

But there were times when she felt as if something was missing. Something…

She was just hot, April told herself. Hot, bored and a victim of cabin fever.

Setting down the stack of mail, she moved toward the open stairs in the rear of the post office. The living quarters were upstairs. She, Max and June had grown up there, living with Gran. Now only Gran still called it home, even though April had tried time and again, if not to lure her away, to at least buy her a small house of her own. Gran wouldn't hear of it.

"Don't want to get used to anything new at my age, except maybe a man," Gran had said with a wink. "You keep your money and buy a house for yourself."

And that was that. Telling Gran she didn't want a house of her own was out of the question. Gran wouldn't have believed her. She had her own preconceived notions of what people did or didn't want and there was no talking her out of them.

"Gran," April called up the stairs, "is there anything I can get you?"

"No, I'm fine, dear," her grandmother's voice assured her. "Just watching my story. I'll be down to help you as soon as it's over."

April shook her head as she hurried up the stairs to head off her grandmother. The woman had a patent on stubbornness. They'd waltzed around this argument every day since she'd arrived. The first day had been the most difficult, but April hadn't fooled herself into believing that she had won the war, just tiny skirmishes here and there.

"No, you won't," April informed her, entering a tiny living room filled to overflowing with knick-knacks that had taken more than six decades to accumulate. April seriously doubted that Gran threw out anything, convinced that the moment she would, a need for the item, no matter how obscure, would arise. "If you remember, the reason I'm here, playing solitaire with all those envelopes, is so that you can rest—and sensibly see your way clear to going to the hospital in Anchorage for—"

Lying on the sofa, Ursula Hatcher waved a small hand in the air to push away the words she knew were coming. "Stuff and nonsense," she proclaimed. "Bunch of children playing doctor, poking at me for no good reason." She raised her chin, tossing her gray-streaked faded red hair over her shoulder. "My heart's fine. It's just a little tired, but it has a right to be. It's been working nonstop for sixty-nine years without a vacation. You'd be tired, too, if you'd worked that hard," she insisted staunchly.

April reached over to adjust the black-and-yellow crocheted throw draped over her grandmother's legs. "That's just the point, Gran—" April began.

Ursula finished adjusting the throw herself, then cocked her head, listening. "Is that the doorbell downstairs?"

April pinned her with a look. Her grandmother was a great one for diversions when she didn't like the subject under discussion. "Whoever it is down there will keep, Gran. They can't be in any sort of a hurry if they're living in Hades.''

"Think you know everything, don't you, child?'' Ursula began digging her knuckles in on either side of the sofa, giving a masterful performance of a person struggling to get up. "It's a postmistress's duty to be there when someone walks into the post office. But that's all right, dear, you're busy. I'll go—''

April struggled to keep from laughing. Her grandmother was ruining her attempt at being stern with her. Very gently, she pushed the older woman back against the mound of pillows she'd personally fluffed up this morning.

"God, but you are good at dispensing guilt,'' she informed her grandmother. The older woman smiled in response. "Stay put, you hear me? I'll go down and see who it is.''

"That's my girl.'' Settling back, Ursula beamed, satisfied. She watched her oldest granddaughter cross to the stairs, affection welling up within her. April was a good girl, if somewhat misguided. "April—''

One foot on the stairs, April stopped to turn around. "Yes?''

Feeling slightly awkward, Ursula lowered her eyes and picked at the yellow-and-white daisies crocheted within the throw. "Did I ever tell you how much I appreciate your coming back to mind the store?''

April's smile broadened. "Yes, Gran, you told me. And you know I'd do anything for you.''

"I know—'' She strained to listen for the sound of movement downstairs. "So go see who it is.'' She raised herself up slightly, so that her voice would follow April down the stairs. "And if you don't know where to find something—"

"You're right here to tell me," April called back, finishing a statement she had heard over and over again growing up. Unlike their far frailer mother, Gran had always promised to be there for them, to show them the way no matter what. And she had. April and her siblings had come to believe that Gran was going to go on forever. Being confronted with a different kind of scenario was difficult to come to terms with. "Yes, I know."

April looked around the small outpost as she reached the bottom of the stairs. As if she couldn't find absolutely everything there was to find in this room within a matter of seconds, she thought. If the post office were any smaller, her claustrophobia would have kicked in.

As it was, the room that housed all the incoming and outgoing mail for Hades could be referred to as small with just cause. She could turn the whole area upside down in a matter of mere minutes if she wanted to.

Gran's hearing was as good as ever, she thought. Someone had entered the post office while she'd been upstairs. The small bell attached to the door hardly made a sound worth listening for, but Gran was apparently still tuned in to it.

"May I help you?"

Shoving her hands into the back pockets of her faded jeans, April addressed the words to the back of a head she didn't immediately recognize. When the man turned around, she found she didn't recognize his face, either. She had to admit that it felt a little unusual not knowing the man. Before she'd left Hades, there hadn't been a face she didn't know, at least on sight.

She would have remembered this face.

With the trained eye of a professional photographer, she studied him quickly from head to toe. He looked to be several years older than she was, but at the same time, he had a face that appeared as if it would remain perpetually youthful even in old age. He had the kind of eyes, blue and intense, that would twinkle well into his nineties.

They were twinkling now as they took slow, careful measure of her. She could almost feel them passing over her body.

She knew the type. Handsome, charming, and as trustworthy as a barrel of snakes after a nine month fast. She'd met more than a few of those in her travels. Men like that made an exhilarating date for an evening, but after that, their charm wore thin. As did any promises they might make in the heat of the moment. Just like her father.

She had no use for that type of man.

Still, she couldn't help wondering who this man was and what had brought him to such a sleepy little place as Hades. It wasn't as if Hades was exactly on anyone's beaten path and it definitely wasn't a place someone would happen on as they were passing through, at least not in this century. A hundred and fifty years ago, prospectors with dreams of getting rich quickly would ride into town, eyeing the hills that were directly behind it. But that hadn't happened for close to eighty years if she was to believe the stories Gran had told them.

* * *

For the first time since arriving in town yesterday, James Quintano, Jimmy to all his friends, found his appetite whetting. Not that he'd arrived in Hades to have his appetite even mildly aroused. He'd come because Alison was here and he'd promised to return to visit his sister and her husband ever since he'd boarded the plane right after her wedding. Hades wasn't a town a man would come to look for a fling or a pleasurable interlude. There was a different breed of people here. Decent people who worked hard and played even harder because those times were precious and rare.

It was also a town, he'd quickly realized, where a man had his work cut out for him if he wanted female companionship of any kind. Alison had told him the odds were something like seven to one against him. Not that he'd ever had a hard time finding willing women. He had a hard time *not* finding willing women. It had been that way for him ever since he'd found puberty a little after his eleventh birthday. He'd grown tall early, began shaving early, and discovered love early. The birds and the bees had had nothing on Mary-Sue Taylor.

Thoughts of Mary-Sue and her successors faded from his mind, as did the woman who was to have accompanied him on the Alaskan cruise before fate in the guise of an apparent family emergency had stepped in.

Habit had him glancing at the blonde's left hand. He found it encouragingly unadorned.

Finished with his appraisal, Jimmy smiled and answered her question. "I certainly hope so."

And then he saw her wrist. His initial scrutiny had

missed that because she'd had her hands tucked into her back pockets, making her jeans strain against her torso and distracting him. Now he saw that there was a makeshift bandage wrapped around her left wrist. One that looked as if it was about to come undone with the very next movement she made.

He nodded at it, coming forward. "What happened to your wrist?"

She looked down at it grudgingly, the stranger's question bringing with it a fresh wave of pain. She'd been trying to put herself beyond that. It was an injury sustained this morning because, as always, she had been moving too fast. But fast was the only tempo she knew. Away from Hades, there was always so much to do that moving fast was a necessity to staying on top of things. Her mind elsewhere, she'd brushed too close to the skillet and been awarded a red badge of courage in the form of a wide, angry blister.

"Nothing. Just a case of a frying pan not moving out of my way," she said with a careless shrug.

As she reached for the pile of envelopes she'd abandoned earlier, the bandages began to loosen in earnest, coming completely undone.

"I can take a look at that for you," Jimmy volunteered, already reaching for her hand.

Instinct, both inbred and acquired, had her pulling her hand away. Suspicion creased the brow beneath her wayward bangs. "And just why would you want to do that?"

He didn't usually meet with resistance when he reached for a woman's hand. Jimmy's smile widened. "Well, for one thing, I'm a doctor."

Chapter Two

April looked suspiciously at the tall, darkly handsome man standing in front of her, still keeping her wrist very much to herself. Medical treatment in Hades came via Dr. Shayne Kerrigan and, recently, his nurse, Jean-Luc's wife, Alison. Shayne had been trying, unsuccessfully, to lure another doctor to Hades ever since his brother, the only other doctor within a hundred-mile radius, had left town to follow his heart's dream—a woman named Lilah who had a wandering soul. Shayne had begged, pleaded and cajoled would-be seasoned physicians and doctors fresh out of medical school to no avail. The idea that one would suddenly just pop up in the middle of town without fanfare and an abundance of rumors preceding him, rumors Gran was always the first to be privy to, was completely beyond belief.

Wariness infused by her wanderings in the city took hold. April eyed the tall, muscular man carefully.

"You mean, you want to play doctor, don't you?"

The stranger's smile widened, becoming even more unsettlingly seductive and convincing April that she'd hit the nail right on the head about him. This was no doctor, this was an opportunist at the very least.

"After all the money my brother invested in medical school, I'd better be able to do more than just 'play' doctor." He took another step toward her. "I'd damn well better be able to be one."

The suspicion didn't abate. As far as she was concerned, there was nothing about Hades that would lure a person to come visit it. Hades wasn't known for anything, had no natural wonders to offer in exchange for the hardship of seeking it out, and it was as far off the usual route as was humanly possible without falling off the edge of the earth.

Yes, the coal mines were still productive, and nicely so, but if the man's hands were any indication, the only kind of physical work he had probably ever engaged in was ridding women of their outer clothing. And quickly, too, no doubt.

April raised her chin, tucking her hand behind her back. "What's a doctor doing in Hades?"

"Visiting," he answered succinctly. Why was she so skittish? Jimmy wondered. It was just her wrist he was offering to examine, not the rest of her. Although that would undoubtedly be richly rewarding. "I won't charge you."

A glint of anger highlighted the suspicious light in her eyes. "For what?"

Had she lost the thread of the conversation? She didn't strike him as the simple type, but looks were deceiving, even mouthwatering ones such as hers. "For looking at your wrist."

She snorted, retreating behind the huge, scarred oak desk that had belonged to Gran's father. Mail was still scattered along its surface. She had work to tend to and this was wasting time.

"Good, and I won't charge you for looking at yours," she retorted.

Although, all things considered, April secretly allowed, the stranger's wrist would have been the very last thing she would think to look at. The rest of him was a good deal more interesting and arresting than his wrist. Apart from a handful of men, her brother included, the male population of Hades would not have stopped any hearts. This man certainly would.

Stop hearts and set pulses racing, and she had a feeling he knew it, too. He was about a foot taller than she was, with dark black hair and eyes the color of the waters off the cape in the spring. The way he held himself, with an easy, comfortable grace, reminded her of one of the Native Americans who'd come into the post office when she was a little girl. Gran had told her he'd once been a chief of a tribe that had since died out. To her, the man had seemed larger than life.

That was undoubtedly what this man was, too, larger than life. Except in his case, that description would involve his own view of himself.

Well, she had better things to do than to stroke his ego. Deliberately, she looked down at the mail on the desk.

As he watched the woman in front of him, Jimmy's grin widened a little more. She had spirit, no question about it. He liked that. There was nothing duller than a woman who just fell into his arms. Ever since he could remember, he'd always enjoyed a challenge. It kept him on his toes and made him feel alive.

He leaned an elbow on the desk, as comfortable as if he'd been coming here for years. "You know, you're the first unfriendly person I've met in Hades."

If he was trying to embarrass her, he was going to have to do a lot better than that, April thought. "Good," she sniffed, turning her back on him. "I never liked being part of the crowd."

That had been his first impression of her, Jimmy thought. Someone not part of a crowd. He leaned forward, watching the way her bottom strained against her jeans as she bent over the mail bag. He had a keen knack for being able to cleanly divorce himself from his professional side outside the hospital. And this lady certainly deserved his undivided attention.

"Oh, you might be in a crowd, but you'd never be taken for being part of it. You'd stand out no matter where you were."

April looked at him over her shoulder, her eyes narrowing. "Is that supposed to impress me?"

"No, that's not supposed to do anything," he told her with such unabashed honesty, she could almost believe him. "It's just an observation. So far, we've ascertained that you stand out in a crowd, you're unfriendly—" his eyes flickered to her wrist "—and you wrap bandages worse than a first year medical student."

She opened her mouth to tell him that he and his observations were free to leave the post office at any time, preferably now. But the words never had a chance to emerge as the man took charge of the moment as well as her wrist by taking the end of the bandage and deftly unwrapping it.

April caught her lower lip between her teeth to keep the startled yelp of pain from escaping her lips.

Pulling her hand out of his grasp would prove to be hurtful, so she left it where it was. Instead she glared at him. "Just what do you—"

The wound appeared to be first degree and didn't look infected. Still, he bet it smarted more than a little. "That's rather angry-looking."

That wasn't the only thing, she thought indignantly. Just who the hell did he think he was? "You want to see angry-looking, just raise your eyes a little, mister. Just what do you think—"

The door swung open behind them. "Jimmy, what's taking you so—" The woman entering the post office stopped abruptly as the sight registered. "Oh, I should have known." A dimple melded into her expression. "Can't let you out of my sight, can I?"

Startled, April looked up to see Alison LeBlanc crossing to them. The dark-haired woman she'd met briefly when she'd gone to see Dr. Kerrigan about her grandmother flashed a rueful smile at her.

Seeing them side by side, April was struck by the similarities between the two people in her grandmother's post office. Although Alison was a good deal shorter, their coloring and the way they held themselves was almost startlingly identical.

April looked from one to the other. "Are you two related?"

Her would-be healer laughed. "Only by the cruel whimsy of fate." With one hand still firmly holding April's, he wrapped his arm around Alison's slender shoulders and gave her a quick hug. "This is my baby sister." There was teasing affection in his eyes as he regarded Alison for a moment. "She's turned out rather nicely, all things considered."

Alison shot him a withering look that somehow still managed to give the impression of affection. "If you mean considering that you were my brother, you're dead-on. I turned out nicely thank-you-very-much despite you, not because of you."

A faint pang drifted through April. This, she thought, she was familiar with. Or at least she had been before she'd moved away. It was the kind of relationship she'd had with her own two siblings, especially with Max. There were times when she truly missed it, though she would admit that to no one because to do so would mean she was vulnerable. If there was one thing she refused to be in any manner conceivable, it was vulnerable. She knew what vulnerability did to a woman.

Alison looked at her apologetically. "I'm sorry, I hope Jimmy hasn't been bothering you. I just sent him out to get the office mail. I should have realized that once he got a good look at you, he'd forget what he came for and try to charm you the way he does every other woman he encounters."

Just as she thought. The man was all flash, no substance. April congratulated herself on her perception.

Rather than look annoyed at having his game plan revealed, the way April would have expected, Jimmy merely laughed.

"I wasn't trying to charm her, I was doing a consultation." To prove it, Jimmy raised the now bandageless wrist he was holding. "The lady seems to have injured herself."

Alison quickly examined the wound. "I've got some ointment for that at the clinic."

"Gran's got some in her medicine cabinet," April countered, indicating the upper floor with her eyes.

"Make sure you put it on," Alison advised. "What happened?"

"Nothing to merit all this fuss." Thoroughly embarrassed now, April tucked her wrist behind her back again. She changed the subject before Alison felt compelled to pursue the matter. "So I take it he's really your brother?"

"Until I can find someone to take him off my hands, yes. He's here visiting me."

Jimmy nodded to confirm his sister's statement, his eyes still on the tempting postmistress who wouldn't give him a tumble. "I wanted to see firsthand just what it is that keeps her here, other than Jean-Luc and that stubborn streak of hers that never lets her admit she's wrong even when she is."

Alison pursed her lips in a mock frown. "It's a family trait."

Jimmy was quick to agree. "Right, our sister Lily has it, too."

Beneath that devil-may-care attitude there wasn't a more stubborn member of the family than Jimmy, Alison thought. It was Jimmy who made a point of volunteering his time at homeless shelters, telling none of them. She would have never known if she hadn't accidentally seen him at a shelter herself. The only notoriety he wanted was that of a playboy, but he was far deeper than that. He had a heart that cared and which was every bit as important as his skilled surgeon's hands. But that was the part of him he wanted no one to know.

"Like you don't," Alison replied.

He made his appeal to April, not his sister. "I am the soul of reasonableness."

Alison merely sighed, shaking her head. She turned to April. "If you give me Shayne's mail, we'll be out of your hair," she promised.

It struck April as odd to have the doctor referred to so familiarly, but then she'd forgotten the townspeople's penchant. Everyone in Hades was on a first-name basis with everyone else.

"Right here." Reaching over the counter to the tallest stack, she pushed it toward Alison. "There might be more." April glanced at semifull sack on the floor. "I haven't finished sorting today's pouch yet."

"Because of the hand," Alison concluded.

April spared Alison's brother a look that said it all. "Because I was interrupted."

If there was a mild accusation in that statement, Alison seemed to ignore it. She merely smiled easily and glanced affectionately at her brother. There was no mistaking the pride in her eyes. "You'll find that Jimmy does that a lot."

That sounded ominously like a promise to her. Or

at the very least, a premonition of things to come. "Why, is he staying on?"

The next question that came to her lips, if the response to the first was affirmative, was "Why?" but she told herself that it was none of her business. If Alison's brother actually was a doctor, having him here would certainly be a welcome relief to Shayne. If her visit to the clinic had been any indication of the way things normally went there, Hades's only physician was completely overworked.

"Just until my ship sails," Jimmy informed her blithely. "Cruise ship," he interjected when the quizzical look on April's face remained. "I'm just here for two weeks." It occurred to him that he hadn't even given her his name—or gotten hers. "James Quintano." Leaning over the counter, he put his hand out toward her.

April paused a moment before finally placing her hand in his. With Alison watching, she couldn't very well remain aloof, although it might do the man some good to see that there were women who didn't fall into his lap just because he was good-looking.

"April Yearling."

Jimmy withdrew his hand. She had a firm handshake. He got the feeling April wanted him to know that she wasn't some frail little thing despite her diminutive size. His eyes held hers for a moment.

Message received.

"Well, now that we're introduced, you'll have to come to my party."

"Party?" April looked at Alison questioningly.

"Luc thought it might be a good way to take care

of the introduction en masse if we just invited everyone to the Salty,'' Alison explained, referring to the saloon that both her husband and his cousin, Ike, owned. The saloon, which Ike initially operated and eventually coaxed Luc to become partners in, had been the first venture of many. Now they owned the general store, Hades's only movie theater and the hotel, as well. The benevolent entrepreneurs were determined to build Hades up to entice the younger generation to remain once they reached eighteen. ''It's tonight.''

It wouldn't have mattered what day it was. April shook her head, reaching for another stack of mail inside the sack. ''I'm not sure I can get away.''

Jimmy squatted until his face was level with hers. ''I'll take it as a personal insult if you don't show up.''

Her eyes narrowed. He'd just made up her mind for her. ''I'll keep that in mind.''

There was a storm brewing here. Alison could read the signs well. Wrapping one hand around her older brother's arm, she began to lead him out of the building.

''We'll get out of your hair,'' Alison told her, giving Jimmy a hard tug.

Jimmy let himself be dragged off. ''Until tonight,'' he called over his shoulder.

''Until hell freezes over,'' April muttered under her breath as she got back to her sorting.

''Of course you'll go,'' Ursula told her firmly when she'd mentioned the party later that day and her intentions of not attending. Kindly hazel eyes pinned

April where she stood in the crowded living room. "And you'll have a good time, too."

Oh, no, she wouldn't, especially not if the so-called guest of honor was there. April began to move around the room, straightening things in a hopeless battle for order amid chaos.

"Gran, I came back to help out in the post office and to talk you into going to the hospital in Anchorage. I did not come back to attend any feeble little gatherings at the Salty Dog Saloon for some pompous, would-be playboy doctor."

She worried her, this one, Ursula thought. She'd been so hurt by first her father's abandonment and then her mother's withdrawal. There was no question in her mind that April had always been tough on the outside, but it was the inside that truly concerned her. Inside, Ursula was certain, was a hurt, frightened little girl who needed to be coaxed out and loved.

"No, that's just a bonus, I'm sure," Ursula told her cheerfully.

April set two Hummel figurines, a shepherd and his lady, equidistantly apart on a small shelf. "I'm not."

"April."

Her grandmother's suddenly weakened voice had April turning around to look at her. Ursula's hand slipped dramatically over her chest, her fingers spreading over her heart.

Ursula sighed deeply. "I'm an old woman, my heart can't take all this arguing and dissent."

April knew an act when she saw one and, happily, this was one. She moved closer to her grandmother. "You're a semiold woman who likes to manipulate."

Ursula let her hand drop, shaking her head in despair. "I should have raised you to be more respectful of your elders."

"You raised me fine." Bending, April brushed a quick kiss to the silky, weather-lined cheek. "You raised me to see through charades and con artists and golden-tongued men."

That hadn't been her doing. That had been in response to her father's actions. Ursula's heart ached, but for a reason that had nothing to do with medical conditions and terminology written in doctors' journals.

"Not every man is out to break your heart, April. What happened to your mother—"

Instantly, April's chin shot up. A warrior on constant guard. "Is never going to happen to me."

Ursula reached for her granddaughter's hand and held it in hers. "I'm glad, child, but that shouldn't have the price tag you're attaching to it." Her eyes searched April's face, looking for a sign, a chink that would let her break through. The girl was so adamant about not being hurt that she wasn't allowing anyone into her life. "It shouldn't prevent you from enjoying yourself. The years go very fast, April. Faster than any of us can imagine. I don't want you standing at the end of your life, whispering, 'If only I'd done things differently.' April, honey, I don't want you to have regrets."

Then they were agreed, April thought. "Neither do I."

But Ursula shook her head. "I meant about not living life."

Gently, April disengaged her hand from her grandmother's. The next moment she was straightening things again, unable to remain still. Unwilling to allow her choices to be examined this way. "I am living life, Gran. I'm out there every day, living."

But Ursula knew better. For all her sophistication, all her potential and promise, April was fleeing life. "You're out there every day, snapping pictures, capturing *other* people living. You can't do it by proxy. You've got to do it yourself. Sometimes you've got to put up with pinched toes to break in the best pair of shoes you'll ever own."

She might have jumped from a plane to photograph a sky-diving couple getting married, but there were some risks April refused to take. The one her grandmother was talking about was one of them.

"What if those shoes never break in right?"

Ursula could only smile, remembering her own short-lived first marriage. Jake hadn't left by choice. A fishing accident had taken him from her. But the heartache had been the same. "Wearing them for a little while's still better than never wearing them at all and going barefoot."

April put down the tiny glass figurines she'd started to line up in a row and turned to look at her grandmother. It was not in her to say no to the woman for long. "You're not going to give up until I go, are you?"

Knowing the victory was hers, Ursula smiled. "When have I ever given up?"

April laughed, sitting on the edge of the sofa, beside Ursula's throw-covered feet. "You have a point."

"I always do." Ursula threw off the cover and swung her legs to the floor.

April rose to her feet, staring. "What are you doing?"

"Well, I'm going, too," Ursula declared. "I've always enjoyed having a good time—and I always have a good time at the Salty."

April thought of the saloon. The men there could get pretty rowdy. And there'd be dancing, she would be willing to bet. She looked at her grandmother suspiciously. Could this whole thing have been a ruse? "What about that heart of yours not being able to take it?"

"That's only when it comes to arguing and dissent. It can take a good time just fine." Ursula winked. "I hear Yuri Bostovik's going to be there." April could have sworn she saw stars in her grandmother's eyes. "He's always been partial to me."

April's mouth dropped open. She'd never thought of her grandmother as having a life outside the post office. "Gran, you're sixty-nine—"

Ursula nodded as she shuffled off toward her bedroom. "And not getting any younger. My point exactly."

April paused, debating. Her immediate reaction was to bully her grandmother into staying in bed, but happiness counted for something in the scheme of things, especially when it came to well-being.

Wavering, she gave in. She supposed it wouldn't do all that much harm. "All right, we'll go for a little while and then I'll bring you home."

That wasn't the way it was going to be if she had

anything to say about it, Ursula thought. She fixed her oldest grandchild with a look meant to establish the order of things between them. She still made the rules.

"I'll go for a little while and then Max'll bring me home. You're going to stay at the Salty."

"And do what?" April wanted to know. "I don't really like beer."

"So?" Ursula's small shoulders rose and fell. "Don't have beer. There're other things to drink at the Salty besides beer. And I'm sure you'll find something to occupy yourself with." Her knowing smile widened. "If you're lucky."

Because it was Gran, April surrendered. For the time being. "You're positively wicked, Gran."

"Only if Yuri gets lucky tonight, dear, only if Yuri gets lucky. Now go," she coaxed. "Get prettier."

April shook her head, watching her grandmother hurry off to do the same.

Chapter Three

Unlike the near-stagnant air, the ocean of noise within the Salty Dog Saloon that evening ebbed and flowed around April, allowing her to pick out a word here and there as she slowly made her way through the teeming crowd of eighty percent wall-to-wall men. She'd elected to come essentially wearing what she'd had on earlier: changing to a blouse, but staying in her worn jeans. She saw no reason to dress up. It wasn't that kind of a party. People in Hades held comfort in high regard.

April looked around. It wouldn't have really mattered what she'd worn. The odds were definitely in her favor, had she been inclined to play that sort of a game. But she wasn't. Looking over the crop of available men was the furthest thing from her mind, except in a remote, analytical sort of way.

She took stock of the scene, seeing it through the eyes of a photographer rather than as a former native who'd made good her escape.

It had been a long time since she'd actually seen so many men in one place at one time. A fragment of a memory nudged at her, blooming in her mind until she'd captured all of it. The last time she'd seen a gathering the likes of this had been here, right after her graduation from high school. She was the first in her family to finish the twelfth grade. Gran had insisted on throwing a party to celebrate the occasion and since the small living area above the post office barely housed the four of them, much less anyone else, Gran had prevailed on the owner of the Salty to hold it here. It hadn't belonged to Ike and Jean-Luc at the time, though they had worked here.

All April really remembered about the party was that she'd been consumed with the thought of finally being able to leave. Not the Salty or Hades, but the area. Alaska. All of it. It had been the only thing on her mind for years. Ever since that morning she'd woken up to find her father gone, she'd wanted to leave herself, to spread her wings and soar.

And she had soared. For six years. Flown to all the major cities in the country, to all the places she'd once dreamed of, sitting up late at night in her tiny alcove of a room, poring over the atlas her father had left behind. The out-of-date atlas with its worn, earmarked pages and its places that continued to exist even though they were no longer referred to by the names that were written down between the covers.

Looking at the people around her now, almost all

of whom she recognized, April expected to feel like an outsider, like someone who had outgrown the place she was visiting. If nothing else, she'd seen more of the world and of life than most of the people here.

Even so, the feeling wasn't quite there. These people she'd been so quick to erase from her life didn't treat her as if she didn't belong. Instead, they behaved as if she had only momentarily stepped out, but was back now. It was an absurd thought because she wasn't back. She was just here temporarily and would be gone again very soon. The sooner, the better.

She saw Yuri Bostovik over in the corner, his gray hair comically parted in the middle and slicked back. The moment he saw her grandmother, he made a beeline for her. Even in this light, she could see Gran blushing—as if she hadn't spent the past hour planning on just how to greet the man. Gran had buried three husbands and still acted as if love was just around the corner for her. The woman was incredible.

April continued sidestepping people and nodding greetings, trying to reach the bar. What surprised her was that along with her detached, analytical feeling was a tiny prick of something she had trouble identifying.

Or maybe it was that she didn't want to identify it. Nostalgia had no place here, in Hades. Not for her. The very idea was ridiculous. Nostalgia came when you remembered something fondly. There was nothing to feel nostalgic about when it came to her past. She'd never liked it in Hades, had always found it lacking. Other than an attachment to Gran, Max and June, there was no reason for her to feel anything at all about this piece of tundra.

So what was this odd feeling that persisted in rambling around inside of her?

"Is this a private smug moment, or can anyone horn their way in?"

The question, whispered against her ear, nearly made her jump. The warm breath that had accompanied it lingered on her skin, throwing her concentration completely off.

Turning, she found that Alison's brother was at her elbow. Jimmy had a frosty mug of beer in each hand, holding them close to his chest to keep from spilling the contents.

She eyed the mugs before looking up at him. Even in the dim lighting from the chandeliers, his eyes were intensely blue. She felt a ripple of excitement wash over her. "Two-fisted drinker?"

Hunching in against her, he seemed to move in closer without physically taking a step. "No, actually this one's for you."

With a human wall suddenly at her back, there was nowhere for her to go. She stifled her impulse to get away. "Me?"

Jimmy nodded. "I spotted you when you walked in with your family. Me and every other male in the room who's breathing," he added with an easy smile that would have broken down a lesser woman's defenses. He held the mug in his right hand up to her. "Thought you might want something to drink."

She'd never really cared for beer, but April supposed it would be rude to refuse the drink so she ac-

cepted the mug. That he included himself in the group
rather than go out of his way to single himself out for
her benefit surprised her. But then, she'd learned that
men were never easy to read.

"Thank you," she murmured.

"So—" he clinked the side of his mug against hers
lightly "—what are you being so smug about?"

She raised her chin defensively. "I'm not being
smug."

He felt a sudden, uncontrollable desire to nibble on
that chin, but held himself in check. This lady required
kid glove treatment. "Yes, you are," Jimmy quietly
corrected. "There was a smug look in your eyes just
now, when you were looking over the people in here."
He studied her for a moment before taking a sip of
his beer. "This your first time back at the Salty?"

It struck her that he sounded as if he were a Hades
native. That was a laugh. A man like Dr. James Quintano couldn't stay in a place like this for more than a
couple of weeks, if that long. She had a feeling Alison's brother would probably cut his vacation short
rather than remain here for the duration. He seemed
like the type who needed a regular dose of excitement
in his life. Someone who needed a party every night.
The only kind of excitement Hades had to offer usually involved natural disasters or fires.

"Yes," she finally answered because he still
seemed to be waiting for a response.

Jimmy took another, longer sip of his beer, his eyes
never leaving her. He liked watching the way her
breasts rose and fell beneath her peasant blouse with

each breath she took. "Luc said you've been away for seven years."

"Six years," she corrected, surprised that Jean-Luc had even noticed her absence. Alison's husband was so laid-back, she hadn't expected ordinary events to make any impression on him. Her departure had been without fanfare, as had her return. "But right now it feels more like six days," she muttered out loud, looking around.

"Homecomings have that effect," he agreed.

Someone bumped into April from behind and pushed her into him. An amber wave rose from her mug and Jimmy found himself being liberally christened with the beer he'd just handed her.

Amused, slightly embarrassed, she looked at the resulting mess. "Oh, I'm sorry."

Jimmy brushed a few golden droplets away from his shirt, but the rest were quickly being absorbed by the dark blue material, creating an irregular-shaped stain on his chest.

Grinning, he shrugged it off. "No harm done." He looked at the throng of people behind her. It appeared as if everyone in Hades and the surrounding area had somehow managed to pack themselves into the saloon. "But I think we might want to step out of range." With his hand against the small of her back, he steered April toward another section that was only slightly less crowded.

April glanced across her shoulder toward where she'd last seen her family, all the way over on the other side of the saloon. Max had disappeared, as had June. Only Gran was there with Yuri. Looking up, the older woman made eye contact with her and smiled, nodding.

She knew that look. It was approval. Gran had never been stingy with hers, but this time her approval had found the wrong mark. April shook her head vigorously before looking away.

Jimmy noted the exchange. He bent his head toward her to be heard. "Is that your grandmother?"

April wrapped her hands around the mug and, wrinkling her nose, took a sip before answering. Though she wasn't sure why, she suddenly found herself in need of fortification herself and this would have to do. "Yes, that's Gran."

He could just barely pick up the affection in her voice. Seeing as how she was trying hard to appear removed, she had to care a great deal for the older woman. "Luc told me a lot about her. She sounds like a wonderful woman."

"She is." April turned her attention back to the man who seemed determined to remain with her. It was a lot less disconcerting to look at him than to feel his breath on her neck. "You seem to have gotten a great deal of information out of Jean-Luc. As I recall, before I left, if he strung three words together in a sentence every few weeks, we called him chatty."

Jimmy laughed and despite the noise in the saloon, the sound wrapped itself around her like a warm scarf on a cold winter's day. Maybe she'd absorbed more alcoholic fumes than she'd realized, April thought.

"He's loosened up some, being married to my sister." Jimmy was just repeating what Ike had told him.

''But he'd have to if only in self-defense. Alison tends to be bossy if she's given her head.''

Alison didn't have the market cornered on that, April thought, glancing at Jimmy. She moved so that he was forced to drop his hand from her back. ''Another family trait?''

Jimmy nodded, downing a little more beer. He set the empty mug on the closest surface. ''My sister Lily's the same way. Could be why she has trouble maintaining a relationship.''

''Meaning that men prefer women who agree with them and who they can walk on.''

The man tending bar slid another full mug his way. Catching it, Jimmy nodded his thanks and took a mouthful. ''Didn't say that.''

Her eyes narrowed. ''But you implied it.''

The look he gave her was innocent. He studied her in silence for a moment. Was she deliberately trying to instigate a fight between them? The thought amused him more than anything else.

''Can't see how. I was just saying that bossing people around never makes for a good relationship no matter which party's doing the bossing, male or female.'' He took another long sip before continuing. ''Never liked walking on people myself. I like a woman who can give as good as she gets.''

Their eyes locked and she had the distinct impression that he was putting her on notice. Though she tried to block it, a small, unidentifiable shiver ran down the length of her spine.

''Then you've come to the right place, Dr. Quintano. The women in Hades definitely aren't pushovers," April told him with a touch of pride. "They've learned to stand up for themselves."

His eyes were touching her, making her uneasy. She became aware of the severe lack of air within the packed saloon. Jimmy's smile was easy, slipping over his lips in slow motion and in direct reverse proportion to the rhythm assimilated by her pulse.

"Glad to hear that."

Yeah, she'd just bet he was. April cleared her throat, then set her mug down on a cluttered table meant for two. "And you're wrong."

Jimmy cocked his head, his eyes on her mouth. "About?"

She shouldn't have had any of the beer. There had to have been something in it. Beer didn't affect her this way, making her head spin and her pulse race, certainly not a few sips.

"Homecomings," she told him stiffly. She realized that she wasn't exactly making sense. She was losing the thread of what she was saying herself. "At least about this being one."

"But this was your home," he pointed out, "and you've come back."

"Just to help out."

He gave another careless shrug. "You've come back. The details don't matter."

Now there she had him. It was her turn to smile confidentially. "Oh, but they do," she corrected with a liberal dose of passion. "Details always matter. They're what makes one thing different from another."

His grin merely served to irk her. "You like to argue, don't you?"

Her chin went up defensively again, and again, he found it tempting. Jimmy seriously toyed with the idea of stealing a kiss, but knew it would just get him slapped royally. He could wait.

"No, I don't like to argue," she contradicted. "I like things to be perfectly clear and up front. No lies, no deceptions, no illusions."

Her words struck a chord. He regarded her thoughtfully for a long moment. "Sounds like someone did a number on your optimism."

She didn't like being analyzed, especially not by a stranger who had no idea what he was talking about. "My optimism is just fine, thank you."

"Good." He placed his mug next to hers on the table. The glass came precariously close to falling before Jimmy steadied it. "Then you won't mind dancing with me."

Maybe she hadn't heard right. "What does one thing have to do with another?"

He wrapped his fingers around her hand. "Your optimism will make you optimistic about my dancing ability."

The next thing she knew, as the protest formed on her lips, she found herself enfolded in his arms. If she strained her ears, she could just about make out that there was a song playing on the classic jukebox that Ike had painstakingly restored. But what that song was, or even the tempo that was presumably playing, was anyone's guess.

Alison's brother, April noticed, took it to be a slow

song. With his hand lightly pressed against her spine, he brought her body closer to his. Closer than she felt comfortable about.

"You're in my space," she hissed against his ear.

He could feel her stiffening. He did his best to lighten the moment and smiled down into her face. "I'm afraid there is no space here, but as soon as there is, I'll be sure to let you have it." The smile widened just a little. "I find this rather cozy myself."

His smile was infiltrating her space even more acutely than his body. She looked around for someone to cut in, but apparently no one else was paying attention to the music. "I'm sure you do."

Curving her hand beneath his, he rested it against his chest. "So what do you do when you're not sorting envelopes?"

She could feel his heart beating beneath her fingertips. Why that made her warm, she couldn't say. Probably had to do with the growing lack of air. "You mean here?"

His eyes held hers. She had hypnotically beautiful eyes, he thought. "Anywhere."

It was definitely too warm in here, she thought. "I'm a photojournalist."

Something independent. He should have realized that. She needed something where she could make her own terms, her own hours. "I'm impressed."

The sway of his hips against hers was far too distracting for her to concentrate on the conversation. "I didn't say it to impress you."

"I know." He liked the way she felt in his arms when she relaxed. Soft, delicate. In direct contradiction to the look in her eyes. "You don't like to impress anyone, do you?"

She tried to shrug and wound up brushing her shoulder against someone's back. "There's no need, as long as I'm happy."

Jimmy was careful to not move their dancing out of the realm of tantalizing and into arousing. He had a feeling she would break away if he did. But having her here, swaying against him this way, was certainly doing a number on him. "Are you?"

"Am I what?"

"Happy."

She could feel her heart constricting slightly and her nerve endings stretching taut. "This conversation's getting way too personal."

He felt her try to pull back, but he held her fast. "How else am I going to get to know you?"

April's eyes narrowed. "Why should you get to know me?"

"Why not?"

Games, he was playing word games. Well, he'd met his match, she thought. She knew how to give as good as she got. "Because in two weeks you'll be gone and with any luck, so will I."

That fit right into his plan. He certainly wasn't looking for anything permanent. If you looked for something permanent, you wound up being disappointed in the end when it broke apart. And in one way or another, it always broke apart. "Yes, but until then, there's all this time just hanging around. We might as well pass it pleasurably."

And she knew just what he meant by that. "Maybe we have a different definition of pleasure."

The dimple in his cheek deepened. "We can explore that, too."

She didn't know whether to be amused or annoyed. What she was, was incredibly warm, bordering on hot. If she didn't get some air soon, she was going to pass out. "You don't give up, do you?"

"Haven't the foggiest how to do that," he admitted readily. "Besides, my brother taught me that anything worth having is worth working for." And that included time with a beautiful lady, he added silently. "If it comes too easily, you might just let it slip through your fingers without realizing it."

The scales began to tip toward amusement. "And your brother's a philosopher."

Kevin would have gotten a charge out of that, Jimmy thought. "A cabdriver. Actually, he owns a fleet of cabs. A small fleet, but the company's his nonetheless." His mouth curved fondly as he managed to turn her around in the tiny space. He liked her surprised expression when she faced him again. "I wouldn't want him knowing I said it, but Kevin's the smartest man I know. The kindest, too." Jimmy glanced over toward where he'd last seen Alison. She was still there, talking to several people from the looks of it. She was standing next to Luc, her arm tucked through his. She looked happy, he thought. It was about time. "He misses Alison." He looked back at April. "Kevin raised her after our parents died. You might say he raised all of us."

"All?" How many of them were there? And were

they all glib, like him? Alison didn't seem to be, but it was too soon to tell. She'd only exchanged a few sentences with her.

"My two sisters and me. I never realized how much he gave up to do that." Jimmy grew serious for a moment, looking back. "Kevin could have had a regular life of his own, dated, gotten married, the usual. Instead he stayed home, put all of us through school, made sure we toed the line and became decent people."

April caught her bottom lip between her teeth. "So how disappointed in you is he?"

It took him a second before he realized she was joking. There'd been a kernel of truth in that. "Not anymore. My wild days are behind me."

Wild, that wasn't quite the word she would have used to refer to him, but it was close enough. "That's not the way Alison made it sound."

Enjoying the company of an ever changing parade of women was harmless compared to the rebellious teenager he'd once been. "I meant as in giving Kevin grief."

Her eyes held his. "So now it's just women you give grief to?"

She was deliberately trying to bait him. Getting a kick out of it, Jimmy grinned. "I don't think they'd refer to it as grief. And whatever happens between a lady and me is by mutual consent. I make a point of never staying where I'm not wanted."

April realized she was flirting, but since it was just for tonight, she could see no harm in it. She supposed her ego could use the temporary high. "And just what kind of signals have to go off before you realize you're not wanted?''

"That's easy," he told her. "The lady says go and means it.''

Right, and if she believed that, there was an ice bridge he wanted to sell her. "So if I said go, you would?''

He grinned. "You're forgetting the key part—'and means it,''' he repeated.

He had a loophole. She figured as much. "And that's up to you to decide, isn't it?''

He laughed. "You're getting the hang of it now.''

The record ceased play, taking the music with it. He was loathe to give her up just yet. He had a feeling that if he continued dancing, she'd follow. For the moment she didn't look as if she realized that the jukebox had stopped playing. But her cheeks were flushed and while he'd like to think he had something to do with that, it was probably the close quarters they were in. "Would you like to get some air?''

They weren't that far from the door. Without seeming to move, they'd somehow managed to dance their way to the saloon entrance.

"Actually, that doesn't sound like a bad idea.'' She nodded toward the doorway. "I'll just step out for a minute.''

When he followed her, she raised a quizzical brow. "Can't let a lady go out alone at night.''

Part of the reason she wanted to step outside was to get away from him and that rock-hard body of his. "You can if the lady insists.''

With that, she slipped outside and closed the door behind her.

Chapter Four

The temperature change registered immediately as the night air briskly embraced April, cooling her skin. The temporary heat of the afternoon had gone as if it had never existed, a cold snap settling in. She'd forgotten how cold it could be in Hades despite the calendar.

Running her hands up and down her arms, April looked up at the sky. The stars were out in full regalia, framing a moon that was full and bright. Less than a handful of streetlights dotted the area, their illumination paling in comparison to the moon's.

The last time she'd stood here like this, there hadn't been anything but darkness. This was progress, she supposed. As everything else in Hades, it came slowly.

When she felt a hand gently settle on her shoulder, April jumped and swung around. Her breathing steadied slightly as her eyes looked up at Jimmy's face, still flush from the warmth within the saloon.

The man obviously couldn't take no for an answer.

Her eyes asked him what he was doing out here after she'd said she wanted to be left alone.

"Like she means it," he repeated, echoing his sentiment from only moments earlier.

It took her a second to remember. And then she frowned. "I meant it. What, I didn't sound convincing enough to you?"

In deference to the chill, he buttoned the top two buttons of his workshirt. "Not to my ears." Amusement glinted in his eyes. "Must have been all that noise inside," he told her innocently. He saw that wasn't going down so well. "Where I come from, it's not polite to tell the guest of honor to get lost."

She laughed to herself, thinking of the crowd inside the Salty. "I hate to break it to you, but you're more of the excuse of honor than the guest of honor."

He shrugged, unfazed. "As long as it involves honor, I'm all right with it."

"Oh, and honor means a lot to you, does it?"

The grin abated just a little, his manner growing ever so slightly serious. "It has its place in my life."

Suddenly his serious mood was gone. Jimmy hunched his shoulders against the wind, wondering if he'd seem like a hopeless tenderfoot if he opted to go inside for the jacket he'd left slung over the back of his chair. April seemed to be faring well in just a simple blouse. A simple blouse that was hugging curves guaranteed to make a man's mouth water. The button just at her chest level strained against its hole every time she took a breath. He tried to not stare. His fingers itched to help coax the separation.

Shoving his hands into his pockets only partially for warmth, he looked up at the moon. "So, what does a person do around Hades for excitement?"

"Leave."

He looked at her. "Seriously."

April inclined her head. "Seriously."

Jimmy couldn't tell if she was deadpanning or not. "My sister seems pretty content."

April had made her own judgment about nurse Alison LeBlanc and found herself liking the woman, although they had little in common. "Your sister belongs to that amazing fraternal club of people who give of themselves and feel that they actually have a calling in life to tend to the sick and the needy."

Alison had always been a caretaker, even though she was the youngest. And there was no denying that her heart was in the right place. But Jimmy had a little bit of trouble with April's assessment of the townspeople. He nodded toward the closed door behind them. "That didn't strike me as a needy bunch in there."

April's mouth twitched. "You should see them around closing time." And then the would-be smile faded. "Actually, I meant 'needy' as in needing. My sister June decided to remain in Hades after she graduated. She could have had her pick of careers, but she opened up a car repair shop of all things. Said the place needed one and since she'd always been so handy when it came to fixing things, it was a good match." Her frown indicated what she thought of that idea. "When he was growing up, my brother Max dreamed about joining the FBI. Now he's content to be the only law around here." She shook her head, his decision mystifying her. "Not that there's any crime in Hades in the conventional sense of the word."

Her wording intrigued him. "What's unconventional crime?"

"When Victor, one of the Inuits, kept springing Simon Gallagher's traps so he couldn't catch any beaver." She couldn't help feeling that her brother was wasting his life here, but it was his to waste she supposed. "Max certainly can't keep busy handing out speeding tickets and the last murder here was—" She stopped to think and realized that if there had been a murder in Hades, she certainly had no knowledge of it. "I don't know when."

Jimmy smiled at the scenario she was unconsciously painting for him. He and his family hailed from Seattle where crime was an everyday event. He could think of several people who would more than welcome life in Hades.

He looked at her. "Sounds like a nice place, actually."

"Bland," April corrected firmly. "It sounds bland."

There was nothing bland about facing the hardships he was sure this place afforded. That took courage and fortitude. But he saw no point in getting into a discussion over it with her. So he humored her instead. "And you crave excitement."

She looked out over the terrain, asleep except for

the party in the building behind them. There wasn't much to see and what there was of it was dark. Even the theater was closed. Since everyone in town was at the Salty, there had been no reason to keep the theater open tonight. She could remember all those years, aching to get as far away from Hades as possible.

"What I crave," she told him, "is something with a pulse."

The grin on his lips was warm, inviting as he held up his hand for her to examine. "I have a pulse."

A smile began to bud on her lips. April could only shake her head. He'd gotten her again. "I have to learn to pick my words more carefully around you."

He moved a little closer to her as the wind rose. "Does that mean you'll be around me?"

He was too close, but to back away would imply that she was afraid, or wary, and that wasn't the sort of image she cared to project. So she stood her ground and ignored the feelings taking place inside of her. "There you go again."

He liked the way her eyes snapped, and the way she smelled when the wind shifted, bringing the scent of her perfume to him. Ever since he could remember, he'd always paid attention to women. All women. The pretty ones he paid a little more attention to.

Inspired by the subtle nuances he was picking up, Jimmy decided to make another pitch. "You can't be postmistressing all the time. I mean, a place like this can't get *that* much mail—seeing as how there aren't that many people here. You have to have some free hours, what do you do then?"

Stepping to the side, she moved away from him. "Take care of my grandmother."

A high-pitched laugh reached them from within, escaping through the fraction of an inch where the window sash failed to meet the sill. They turned and April could see her grandmother was standing right next to the window. From all appearances, she was vamping the socks off the gray-bearded man she was with. Jimmy, eyeing Yuri Bostovik, noticed that he looked almost besotted with April's grandmother.

Nothing he liked better than to see seniors enjoying their lives. Jimmy grinned and looked at April. "Looks to me like your grandmother is taking care of herself." More than a touch of admiration mingled with his amusement.

The way April saw it, Gran was doing the exact opposite. She should have been at home, resting, not out at the saloon. The woman had angina, for heaven's sake. But there had been no talking her out of coming. Gran had been insistent. Until this moment, despite Gran's blatant allusions to Yuri, April had thought it was to insure her coming here. Now she wasn't so sure.

She watched the older couple move and meld into the crowd. April shook her head. "Gran's headstrong. She absolutely refuses to let me take her to Anchorage—to the hospital there."

The woman looked healthy enough, even glowing, but Jimmy knew how deceptive appearances could be.

"Can't Shayne treat her? Alison says he's the best." He remembered feigning jealousy when Alison had told him that, but they'd both known he'd been kidding. He hadn't an envious bone in his body. And he knew that while Alison was kind, she wasn't recklessly lavish with her praise. She called them as she saw them.

"I'm sure he is for the common everyday things, but it's her heart—"

"What about her heart?"

Because they'd been preying on her mind ever since she'd received June's letter, the words were out before she realized that she was sharing them. "She has angina and Shayne suggested an angiogram to see if there's any sort of blockage. Her EKG looks good, but an electrocardiogram is almost useless in determining the actual condition of a heart—and she'd been having these pains."

Jimmy wondered how much was true and how much had been fabricated by Ursula Hatcher for April's benefit. From what Alison had told him, he had a hunch the crafty-looking woman on the other side of the pane had exaggerated her condition to get something she wanted—her granddaughter in the area. "What kind of tests have been done?"

Interest mingled in with her suspicion. "What kind of a doctor are you?"

"A good one, I'd like to think." He regarded Ursula's profile with interest before turning back to one that interested him more at the moment. "I can take a look at her for you if you'd like."

"I don't need her looked at, I need her scanned."

Jimmy laughed. "You make her sound like some sort of digitalized cartoon character."

"No, she's a person," April said softly as she

watched her grandmother shamelessly flirt. "A very precious person."

Jimmy watched as moonbeams tangled themselves in April's hair. Urges whispered softly through him. It was hard keeping his mind on the conversation. "She'd have to be, to get you to come back to a place you hate so much."

April didn't like having things presumed about her, or having words put in her mouth. "I never said I hated Hades."

Was she serious? He looked at her expression, clearly challenging him, and realized that she was. Very serious. "In every way but to actually use the word," he contradicted.

She opened her mouth to put him in his place then closed it again, deciding the argument wasn't worth the effort. Not when he was right. It was just that she didn't like having someone read her so well, not a stranger at any rate.

Shrugging, she looked away. "It's just that I find it stifling here, confining."

"Oh, I don't know. When something's unformed like Hades, there's a world of possibilities in that vastness. You can do anything, be anything. It's like a huge empty canvas you can paint on."

He'd said he was visiting, but maybe it was more than that. Maybe he was checking things out. "You sound like somebody who's fixing to make a monumental move."

Not hardly, he thought. He had everything set up for him at the hospital back in Seattle. That had taken some doing. Besides, Kevin was having enough trouble with Alison being so far away. His older brother would seriously flip out if two members of his family were more than an hour away by regular route. Jimmy supposed, after sacrificing so much for them, Kevin felt he deserved to be part of their lives once those lives took shape.

Jimmy shrugged casually. "No, just somebody who's always got his eye out for possibilities."

"I would have thought that someone like you would have restricted his possibilities to women."

"There's that field, too." His grin was wide and it tugged at her, pulling her in against her will. "But not restricted, never restricted."

When he looked into her eyes like that, she found she had trouble thinking. Good thing she'd stepped out for some air when she had. She'd definitely been in danger of light-headedness. "So, where do you practice—medicine, I mean."

"I don't have to practice," he told her, his voice low, moving slowly around her, hypnotizing her. "I have it down pat—medicine, I mean."

April shivered, trying to snap out of the trance she felt herself falling into.

"Cold?"

It was as good an excuse as any. "Yes. Spring here is only a little warmer than winter at times."

Too late she realized it was the wrong thing to say because he slipped his arm around her shoulders, then shielded her against the wind with his body. "Maybe we'd better get you inside."

She'd gotten good at rejecting men who came on to her. She could do a put-down with just a well-aimed glance. There was no doubt in her mind that James Quintano was definitely coming on to her. She could feel it in every bone in her body. But when she turned her head toward him, no words came, no well-honed, belittling glance found its way into her eyes. Instead, she felt a definite pull toward this man she didn't know.

"Maybe," she agreed, her voice hardly above a whisper.

Reaching around her, he put out his hand to push open the door. And wound up wrapping that same hand around her other side instead. Pulling her to him.

He'd meant to be on his best behavior, he really had. But when she looked at him like that, with the moonlight caressing her face and moonbeams getting lost in that tangle of hair that invited his fingers to touch it, he felt something stronger than his good intentions stir within his gut.

Before he quite knew what he was doing, natural born instincts had him cupping her cheek and tilting her face up to his. Had him touching his mouth to hers to break the spell because nothing could taste as good as her lips looked.

He was wrong.

They could.

Maybe it was because he'd been at loose ends ever since Melinda had canceled out on him, begging off from the cruise because of some personal emergency at home that now eluded his brain.

The real emergency, he'd had no doubt at the time, was that she'd had marriage on her mind and he'd had nothing more serious than a pleasant interlude on his.

It wasn't that he had anything against marriage in general, just nothing for it in particular when it came to himself. He reasoned that he saw enough dying at the hospital, he didn't need to be part of something that, no matter what, had a finite lifespan. His parents had driven that lesson home long before he'd ever put on his first pair of scrubs.

But that belief in no way made him monastic. For him, relationships lasted as long as they were mutually beneficial, comforting and light. While he was involved, he could be counted on for emotional support, a kind word and to be summoned in the middle of the night in case of a breakdown—as long as he wasn't on call. Even after a relationship had run its course, he usually remained on good terms with the woman. But he'd made it a rule never to meet the woman's family or to discuss anything more romantically serious than pending plans for the weekend. He didn't believe in committing himself to anything longer than that.

Right now, there was no weekend, no future, no past. Nothing but the moment.

A moment bathed in a feeling so incredible it defied succinct description. And that bothered him. Though he considered himself footloose and independent, he also liked labels. If something was labeled, it couldn't suddenly render a surprise he might find himself unprepared for.

He wasn't prepared for his reaction to April.

Not the degree of it at any rate. He felt his body tighten, as if every sinew was on alert. Poised. Taut.

Slanting his mouth against hers and pulling her

closer still, he deepened the kiss. Layer fell upon layer, wrapping him tightly within.

Like someone desperately trying to follow a path through a blizzard to get home, April was appalled to discover she'd lost her way. Lost it completely and immediately the instant his mouth touched hers. One second, she'd wondered at this strange electricity that danced between them, charging her. The next, she'd found herself cocooned by something that was dragging her down and flowing over her head.

She remembered falling into the river once when she was very young. Victor, a dour-faced, half Native American, half Inuit they'd all believed was completely crazy, had pulled her out. Grabbing her by her hair, he'd managed to pull her to the surface and then swim for shore. To this day, she remembered what it had felt like, going down for the last time. She'd thought she was dying, but it had ceased to be a frightening experience. Disembodied, she had found herself floating between one world and the next.

That was how this felt. Disembodiment. Not quite real.

And yet it was. So real it was almost agonizingly exhilarating.

Her heart pounding, her fingers curled into his hair, she pressed her mouth harder against his. Savoring, enjoying. And determined, with her last breath, to make him remember this as much as she remembered almost drowning.

And then, for self-preservation purposes, because she needed to stop this before it completely obliterated her, April pulled back her head and looked at him.

It took her a second to catch her breath. "What did you do that for?" she demanded.

The lady packed a hell of a punch, he thought. He couldn't remember the last time a slight kiss had turned into a full three-course affair. He found himself fighting the urge to do it all over again. "Have you ever felt like you just had to find something out?"

April struggled for her deepest sounding voice, afraid anything less than that would crack in the middle. "I generally go to the encyclopedia."

His grin was ever so slightly lopsided. He toyed with a strand of her hair.

"They don't have anything like this in the encyclopedia—or on the Internet, either," he added, second-guessing what she was about to say.

No doubt about it, she thought. Educators and scholars probably hadn't come up with a word to fit what had just happened here. Electricity didn't do it justice, but for lack of anything better, it would have to do.

"I think I've had enough fresh air for now," she told him, turning away.

"You still haven't answered my question." His voice followed her into the now comforting warmth of the Salty. Funny how all these people she'd wanted to get away from had suddenly formed a haven for her.

She glanced at Jimmy over her shoulder. Her heart began racing again the moment she did. What was wrong with her? "I wasn't aware that I'd left anything unanswered."

He moved so that he blocked her path. "All right,

let me put this as formally as possible. Will you be my guide while I'm in Hades?''

Because she found herself wanting to spend time with him under any excuse, she said the first thing that popped into her mind. ''Why can't Alison be your guide?''

''She and Shayne are busy almost all the time. I can't just expect Alison to take off just to show me around Hades.''

He had a point, but she had herself to think of. ''There isn't that much to see.''

His eyes narrowed as if he was attempting to get inside her head. ''As a photographer, you can't be serious.''

He made it sound as if she did nothing but take eight by ten glossies of things that wound up being preserved in coffee table tomes which went generally unnoticed by anything except dust.

''I'm a photojournalist,'' she emphasized. ''There're no stories here.''

There were always stories. He'd seen volumes in the eyes of the people who came to him in the emergency room. ''Maybe you just don't know how to look.''

Fire leaped into her eyes, put there by his words and by her own annoying reaction to his closeness. There were things going on in her body that she didn't like. Things such as longing. She didn't want a fling with this man unless it was on her own terms and she wasn't entirely sure if she could dictate them.

''I know exactly how to look. I—'' She stopped, realizing that he was amused and that she was working herself up needlessly. "You're baiting me again, aren't you?"

He had the face of an innocent angel when he looked at her.

"I wouldn't dream of it. But I am asking for that tour." Ursula Hatcher came into his line of vision. She was dancing with Yuri. Or just swaying side to side in reality. "I tell you what, you show me around Hades and I'll examine your grandmother. I'm a surgeon, which means I have a pretty good working knowledge on how the body should and shouldn't work," he added glibly to give weight to the trade. "How about it?"

She knew she wanted to. Giving in, she told herself she had nothing to lose. "All right, I guess it can't hurt. Maybe if both you and Shayne tell her she needs to go get herself looked at, she'll finally listen. God knows she won't listen to me."

"Maybe it's because you're her granddaughter."

"What's that got to do with it?"

"People who are used to being in charge don't like being given advice by the people they've raised, no matter how well intended the advice is. It has something to do with the passing of authority. Seems to me that she's not quite ready to relinquish hers."

April blew out a breath. "You don't know what you're talking about."

"Minored in psychiatry," he told her.

She stopped trying to get by him and glared, hands on her hips. "I don't care if you dated Freud, you don't know what you're talking about." She turned and tried to walk away. Her progress was impeded no matter which way she looked.

Jimmy kept pace and was right behind her. "Freud wouldn't have dated me. He had an Oedipus complex."

That made her laugh. Turning around, she found herself brushing up against him. This time when the electricity came, she allowed herself to enjoy it. "Do you just talk until you wear someone down?"

"Pretty much. How am I doing?"

He'd won the round and she couldn't say that she was actually unhappy about it. "Come around one tomorrow. I'll close the post office early for the day—just for the day."

That was fine by him. If anything longer was in the offing, that would come. Besides, there was only a day less than two weeks to deal with, anyway. And he did find her very appealing and attractive.

"I don't like making long-range plans, either," he told her.

"Good, then." She put her hand out, as if they were sealing a business deal. "It's settled."

He slipped his hand into hers, his eyes promising a great deal more than his words. She felt a deep flutter in the pit of her stomach and ignored it. Or tried to.

"I'll be there at one," he promised.

When Alexander Connors came up behind her to claim a dance, April felt relieved to have an excuse to leave Jimmy's company.

And just a little disappointed, as well.

Chapter Five

Walking into the post office, April flipped on the lights. The bulbs struggled to illuminate the area, creating more shadows than pools of light. It was almost unnaturally quiet. Crossing to the stairs in the rear, April heard nothing but the sound of her own footsteps on the scarred wooden floor.

After six years of being away from Hades, the silence was particularly hard for her to get accustomed to. Even though she always lived alone in the various places she'd been to, the sounds of the city always permeated her apartment, offering the covert comfort that life existed outside the walls that surrounded her. Here the houses were far apart enough that once evening came with its accompanying darkness, sending people into their homes, a silence fell over Hades like a heavy, oppressive snowstorm.

She shivered, trying not to dwell on it or to let it get to her.

She'd left the Salty after being there for the better part of three hours. She'd danced with more partners than she had fingers and toes, renewing old acquaintances and hearing herself tell the same story over and over again. Each new partner had seemed eager to catch up on her life. As if word of mouth hadn't already done that. Her grandmother not only delivered the mail, but single-handedly delivered the news, as well, passing on what people told her.

April was certain that every one of the men who danced with her tonight already knew all about her career, her growing success and that she was unmarried. But they'd asked and she'd told, in abbreviated statements that progressively became shorter and shorter as the evening lengthened. The only thing that had remained the same in her recitation from one end of the night to the other was that she was only here temporarily. Just long enough to get her grandmother on the road to recovery. And then she was taking the first road out of Hades, no offense, but thank you very much.

After she'd finally decided she'd had enough personal narrative and dancing for the evening, she'd looked around for her grandmother. Her intent had been to take Ursula home with her. But her grandmother had been nowhere to be seen. Which meant that Max had undoubtedly taken her home on his way back to his house. They'd already agreed to that earlier.

Flipping the light switch at the bottom of the stairs,

April smiled to herself. There was a time when her younger brother would have closed down the Salty. But that was before he'd ever turned to law enforcement. The responsibility of the office had caused him to call it a night long before the last patron would leave the party. He'd mentioned something to her earlier about needing to be up early tomorrow to complete the monthly report that was due on some bureaucrat's desk in Fairbanks come the beginning of the week.

As unlikely as it seemed, given his rebellious teen years, her little brother had found his niche in the world. As had her sister, April thought.

As had she, she added after a beat, coming to the head of the stairs. But for her, there was this restlessness she couldn't seem to put to bed no matter where she was. This feeling that despite her travels and her career, things remained unsettled in her life.

April couldn't help wondering if Max and June were as restless within the niches they had carved out for themselves as she was within hers.

She shrugged away the thought. She had a career, earning good money at what she loved doing, how much better did she expect things to be?

Better, a small voice whispered within her.

For a moment, while she'd been dancing in that doctor's arms, she'd felt an attraction, a strong pull. And that same small voice inside her had said, *This.* What the hell that was supposed to mean, she had no idea. Probably that she was just tired and hearing things that weren't being spoken.

Even by annoying inner voices.

She thought first of calling up to her grandmother, then decided against it. Undoubtedly, Gran had probably gone straight to bed when she'd come home. It was exhausting being around so many people. She felt a little drained herself.

April paused, thinking. The very fact that her grandmother had left the party early obviously indicated that she was right about being concerned about the older woman. There had been a time when Gran had kicked up her heels with the best of them, dancing, drinking and laughing into the wee hours of the morning. The joke was that she'd buried three husbands because no man could keep up with her. And Gran had done nothing to dispel the notion. She clearly loved that kind of attention.

And everyone, April mused, running her hand along the worn banister, clearly loved Gran. As did she. With all her heart.

She hesitated by the older woman's door, her hand raised to knock. But then, after a moment, she let her hand drop to her side. There was no light coming from beneath the door, which meant that Ursula might have dropped right off to sleep.

Good, she needs her rest.

Turning on her heel, April took the few steps to her room. She was about to go in, but something made her hesitate and she looked over her shoulder at her grandmother's door again. Doubts and concerns began to nudge forward. Gran was probably completely worn out from tonight's festivities. It wouldn't hurt to just look in on her for a second to make sure she was all right. If she was quiet, April thought, she wouldn't disturb Gran at all.

Her own thoughts made her shake her head in amusement. Who would have ever thought she'd turn into such a worrier? Not her. All she'd ever wanted when she was growing up was to be footloose and carefree, moving from place to place without ties, without restrictions. Accountable to no one. But being accountable and worrying about someone were two very different things. Her mother had been neither. Not concerned about the three children she'd brought into the world and certainly not worried about being accountable for their welfare.

If it hadn't been for Gran…

April shook herself free of the thought and returned to her grandmother's door. Very slowly, she turned the knob and eased open the door. She held her breath, hoping that she wouldn't wake the woman up.

She didn't.

Her grandmother wasn't there.

The bed was still made up and hadn't been touched since before they'd left for the party. A quick glance to the left showed April that the bathroom door was open, the room dark and unoccupied.

"Gran?"

There was no answer, just as she knew there wouldn't be. There weren't that many places her grandmother could have been in this small wooden building and she'd already passed through all of them.

Where was she?

April leaned against the door, not knowing what to think. She was sure she hadn't seen her grandmother when she'd left the Salty. Just before leaving, she'd purposely made an entire sweep of the saloon, weaving in and out through the crowd that had begun to thin out, looking for her.

She was almost positive that Ursula Hatcher hadn't been anywhere. Her brother had been nowhere to be seen, either, so April had just assumed he'd taken her home. And since Gran's all-terrain vehicle had been parked out back of the saloon while Max's had been gone, she'd driven Gran's ATV home.

Steely skeins of concern began to knit themselves together in her head. If Gran wasn't at the Salty and she wasn't home, where was she?

Maybe Max hadn't driven their grandmother home, maybe he'd driven her to the medical clinic or the hospital.

Telling herself not to panic, April hurried to the telephone in the living room. She'd tapped out four numbers before the fact that she hadn't gotten a dial tone registered. Mumbling under her breath, April dropped the receiver into cradle then snatched it up again. She held it to her ear and listened. Nothing. The phone was dead. Perfect.

"Progress certainly doesn't like to stick around long in Hades, does it?" Frustrated, she threw the receiver back into the cradle a second time.

Downed lines were not uncommon in these regions. They were a fact of life. She didn't have time to sit around to wait until they came back to life. That could take hours. Or days.

"Rustic charm, my foot," she declared tersely to the empty room, remembering what Jimmy had said to her about the area. "He thinks it's so great, *he* can stay here."

Flying down the stairs, she grabbed the car keys, and quickly she jammed her arms into a jacket and ran down the three steps at the front of the post office. She was going back to the Salty, praying that for some reason, she'd somehow managed to overlook her grandmother and that the woman was still there, wondering what had become of her.

April got in behind the wheel. Her earlier thought came back to haunt her. What if Gran had suddenly taken a turn for the worse while coming home with Max? What if Max had to have her taken to Providence Hospital?

Caught up in the scenario, her heart began to pound. Now that she thought of it, she didn't remember seeing Shayne or his wife at the gathering when she left, either. They were both licensed pilots and flew Shayne's plane regularly, usually to Anchorage for supplies.

Maybe this time they had to leave to fly her grandmother to—

"Damn it, April, get hold of yourself," she ordered angrily. "You sound like some hysterical dimwit. It's going to be fine, just fine." She pressed down hard on the accelerator. "Max would have found some way to get word to you if there was something wrong."

Not over downed power lines, he couldn't, she reminded herself.

She pressed down harder on the accelerator, pushing it all the way to the floor.

Maybe someone at the Salty had seen her grandmother leaving.

* * *

Jimmy had said his good-nights and assured his sister that even a city kid like him could find his way back to her house. It was only a short distance from the Salty. He'd wanted a little time by himself. Being in the midst of teeming humanity usually did that to him. After endless shifts at the hospital, he had made it a practice to go up on the roof to look up at the stars and pretend, for a little while, that he was alone.

For some reason, there was comfort in the heart of the loneliness.

Jimmy heard the vehicle before he actually saw it. The squeal of brakes behind him made him think, momentarily, that he was back in Seattle at the height of rush hour. Or back in school, driving one of Kevin's cabs for pocket money.

Turning around, Jimmy saw April leaping out of a car that looked as if it, quite possibly, was older than she was.

What struck him was the expression on her face.

He'd seen that look before, on the faces of family members accompanying someone being brought into the emergency room, usually in critical condition. Except that she was alone.

Jimmy thought of her grandmother and what April had said about her condition. The man in him that had been admiring the way each deep breath she took sent her breasts straining against the blouse that was framed on either side by her jacket, was instantly sublimated as the doctor emerged.

"What's wrong?"

She hardly spared him a look. "It's my grand-mother—" The words came out breathlessly.

She was hurrying past him. Probably to find Shayne, Jimmy realized.

He grabbed her arm to get her attention. "Heart attack?"

Preoccupied, afraid of her own thoughts, April half turned to look at him. She struggled to bank down the terror. "God, I hope not."

He'd left his medical bag at Alison's, he thought. "What are the symptoms?"

She shook her head, feeling horribly helpless and frustrated. "I don't know what the symptoms are," she snapped at him. "I can't find her."

Confused, he let her arm drop as he stared at her. "What do you mean, you can't find her?"

Her irritation at the question increased and threat-ened to erupt. "I came home and she wasn't there. I thought she'd left the Salty—when I left, I looked for her and didn't see her anywhere so I thought—what am I telling all this to you for?" It wasn't him she was turning to for help. Turning on her heel, she hur-ried into the saloon.

"Maybe to gather your wits together," Jimmy sug-gested, following her inside. He tried to help. "When did you see her last?"

"Here." April plowed her way through the people who were still there, looking from one end of the sa-loon to the other. All in all, it wasn't that big a place. She told herself that she wouldn't have missed seeing one small woman. "When I was with you."

He remembered. "She was with that man then, wasn't she?"

April had to stop and think about who he was referring to. "Who, Yuri?"

"Maybe you should ask him where she went."

She sighed. If she'd been thinking more clearly instead of jumping to conclusions she would have thought of that. "Right."

But Yuri wasn't anywhere to be found, either.

Frustrated, April leaned against the bar. From there, she had a clear view of the entire place. And neither Yuri, and more importantly, her grandmother, was anywhere to be seen. She frowned, turning to Jimmy. "Yuri probably went home early. He's not that young."

Jimmy wasn't so sure. Age was not just something that could strictly be measured in years. He knew thirty-year-olds who acted as if they were on the ancient side of seventy and eighty-year-olds who behaved as if they were twenty.

"Looked pretty young to me," Jimmy commented with a smile. "Looked rather taken with your grandmother, too." A sparkle entered his eyes. "Maybe if we find him, we'll find her."

Her eyes narrowed. She didn't care for where this conversation was heading. "Are you saying that my grandmother is—"

"Not as old as you might think she is," Jimmy interjected. He saw Ike look at him questioningly from behind the far end of the bar, indicating the spigot. He shook his head in reply. He'd had enough beer for the night. "From what I saw, there was still a great deal of life left in the lady. Ike told me earlier that your grandmother outlived three husbands. Legend has it they all died with a smile on their faces."

He was laughing at her grandmother, she thought. "I resent what you're implying."

He studied April a moment to see if she was serious. "Why should you resent my thinking that your grandmother's enjoying herself?" It didn't make sense to him. "Life's hard enough, especially around here, from what I gather. Why shouldn't your grandmother enjoy herself with someone if the occasion arises, so to speak?" He couldn't help the grin that rose to his lips. "I say good for her."

And he meant it. A good relationship, however long it lasted, was hard to come by. Connections were important at any age.

Hands on hips, April looked at him incredulously. "You think my grandmother went to bed with Yuri Bostovik?"

That was a definite possibility. "Or at least to his place."

April shook her head adamantly. This was her grandmother they were speculating about. Gran sorted mail and gossiped. And on occasion, baked badly misshaped chocolate-chip cookies. "She wouldn't do that."

He wouldn't have thought, to look at April, that she would be so vehement in her denial. If he'd had a grandmother who'd found companionship, even fleeting companionship, he would have thought it great. "Do you know where he lives?"

"Yes, I know where he lives." Everyone knew

where everyone lived in Hades. Nothing ever changed, no one ever traded houses.

"Well, then there's only one way to find out if your grandmother is with him, isn't there?"

She didn't particularly like the way his smile teased her.

"She's not there," April insisted with feeling as she walked out of the Salty some ten minutes later. To cover all bases, she'd made the rounds again, asking everyone she came across if they'd seen her grandmother. To her annoyance, Jimmy had remained at her side. As if he had business being there. As if he cared one way or another where her grandmother was.

No one had seen Ursula out of Yuri's company and Nat Rydell told her he thought he'd seen the two of them walk out together. But Nat had trouble seeing his hand at the end of his wrist after he'd had more than one beer April had informed Jimmy when he'd grinned at her, so there was no reason to believe that he'd seen what he'd claimed.

"I'm only going to see Yuri to ask him when he last saw my grandmother," she told Jimmy tersely.

It was colder now than it had been when they'd stepped out earlier. She zipped up her jacket, shoving her hands into her pockets and searching for the car keys.

"Good start," Jimmy acknowledged, nodding his head. He didn't bother hiding the hint of a smile that played along his lips.

She stopped abruptly when she realized he was dogging her tracks. "Where are you going?"

He nodded toward the vehicle he'd seen her drive off in earlier. "With you."

Suspicion nudged at her with pointy horns. "Why?" Finding the key, she unlocked the driver's door.

He stepped around to the passenger side, waiting to be allowed in. "Finding out I'm right usually makes my day. Or night."

She glared at him over the roof of the car. "You're not."

The smile merely widened. He had a hunch he knew people better than she did. There'd been a zest to Ursula that he'd detected even with a window between them. A zest that belonged to a woman who still knew she was desirable. "We'll see."

She pulled open the door. "Look, my grandmother's none of your affair."

"No," he agreed. "But if something has happened to her, I'd like to be there to help—" The serious look evaporated. "Provided it's help she needs and not just applause."

And here she thought he was on the level. There was nothing she hated more than to be taken in. "You're disgusting."

"I'm a realist," he corrected. "And your grandmother, from what I saw, has a real zest for life. As a doctor, I can't help but admire that."

She didn't think it was the doctor in him that was admiring her grandmother's supposed lascivious nature. For a second, April debated just jumping into her car and pulling away. He had no idea where Yuri lived and she could easily be rid of him. But if, for some reason, her grandmother was with Yuri, she actually might need medical attention. Her heart couldn't take what her body might want. Heaven knew there were times her grandmother didn't have the sense of a flea.

Oh, God, this was her grandmother she was thinking about.

April got into the car and then passed her hand over her forehead, feeling the beginnings of a tension headache to end all tension headaches.

With a sigh, she leaned over and opened the passenger door.

"All right, get in. Just don't talk," she warned him.

Jimmy got in, shutting the door. He looked at her as he buckled up. "You worry about your grandmother a great deal, don't you?"

She turned the key in the ignition. "I said, don't talk."

The takeoff was far from smooth and he had a hunch she had done it on purpose. "Just making conversation with my guide, that's all."

She'd almost forgotten about that. "This isn't part of the tour."

"I said I wanted to see Hades. I didn't mean necessarily during the day."

There was something in his voice she couldn't put her finger on, but she knew trouble when she heard it. "During the day is the only time you're seeing Hades if I'm doing the driving. Alison or Luc can show you around at night. Or someone else. Seems to me like you make friends easily enough."

Sitting back, he studied her profile and wondered how much of the tension he saw had to do with her grandmother and how much had to do with him. "Oh, I don't know, I seem to be having trouble convincing you I'm friendly."

He had that straight. She didn't know what had possessed her to agree to showing him around in the first place. "No offense, 'Dr. Jimmy,' but I've seen your kind of friendly and I can do without it."

"Everyone should learn how to enjoy themselves, April."

"When I get the time, I'll look into it."

"When people say that, that's usually the time they need it the most."

She didn't answer him. Maybe there was some truth in what he was saying, but she didn't want to explore it, not when her mind was so preoccupied.

There were lights up ahead coming from the back of Yuri Bostovik's house. Where the bedroom was likely to be. Was that a bad sign?

What's wrong with you? The man's probably getting ready for bed.

God, but she hoped he was getting ready alone.

"He's home," she murmured more to herself than to Jimmy.

She stopped the car and pulled up the hand brake, hard. Without another word to Jimmy, she hurried out, ran to the front door and knocked.

Praying.

Chapter Six

No one answered her knock.

"Maybe they're asleep," Jimmy suggested.

She resented the pronoun. "Yuri lives alone." April didn't bother turning around to look at him. With the heel of her hand, she pounded on the door again. "Yuri, I know you're in there. It's April Yearling. Please, open up!"

"Maybe we'll have better luck if we try throwing pebbles at his window."

She could hear the grin in Jimmy's voice and it only made her more irritated. He wouldn't be taking it so lightly if this was *his* grandmother they were looking for. "They'd have to be boulders, not pebbles," she told him. "The man is partially deaf."

Since she wouldn't turn around, Jimmy moved to lean against the house to see her expression. Except for the moonlight, the area was devoid of light. "Then how do you expect him to—"

"I said partially," she retorted, pounding on the door again. Was this annoying man determined to take apart everything she said?

This time, the door opened. The man Jimmy had seen practically devouring April's grandmother with his eyes and hanging on her flirtatious smile stood in the doorway, looking bewildered and sheepish. His clothes, Jimmy noticed, had the suspicious appearance of being just a wee bit disheveled.

April didn't wait for a formal invitation from Yuri. With the familiar air of someone who had grown up amid these people and had a strong, unspoken connection to all of them, she walked right into his house. A single floor lamp that had been turned on before Yuri answered the door lit the way into his Spartan living room.

Yuri's black eyes darted from April to the man he vaguely recognized and then toward the back of the house.

He cleared his throat nervously. "I did not expect to see you here," he told April. "Is there something I can be doing for you?"

Yes, you can tell me where my grandmother is. April dragged a hand impatiently through her hair, trying not to let her thoughts run away with her. "I'm sorry to barge in like this, Yuri, but you're the last person to have seen her."

"Her?"

The comical way Yuri echoed the single word had

Jimmy biting his tongue not to laugh. He knew neither party would appreciate his sense of humor right now.

April nodded. For the first time, she took a good look at the old man before her. He had a trim gray beard and his hair was a bit shaggy at the back—a little like the smirking doctor next to her, now that she thought of it. Her grandmother liked longer hair in men. She said it gave a woman something to run her fingers through.

April's eyes narrowed as she regarded Yuri. The fact that he was shifting his weight from foot to foot wasn't wasted on her.

"Her," she repeated. "My grandmother."

Jimmy saw a red tinge creep from the top of the old man's cheeks to settle along his earlobes. Since it wasn't hot in the room, he assumed the sudden color was from embarrassment rather than any sudden whimsical behavior on the part of his blood pressure.

He was right, Jimmy thought. They *had* interrupted something. He wondered if there was any way to convince April to just leave. One look at her face gave him his answer.

"Well, yes, I was." Yuri said each word as if he were slowly measuring them out with a spoon.

April could feel her impatience intensifying. "Did you see where she went?"

Jimmy saw the man look at him as if silently asking for help. "Yes."

This was like pulling teeth, April thought, frustrated. The people in Hades were even slower than she remembered. Molasses flowed faster than any of Yuri's sentences.

"Well?" she pressed. "Where did she go?"

Trapped, Yuri looked down at his worn shoes. The voice that finally emerged was hardly audible. "Here."

"What?" April squeezed the single word out of a throat that was closing over. He was right, damn him. The smirking doctor beside her was right.

"Here," he finally told her. "Your grandmother is here."

Since she wasn't retreating of her own volition, Jimmy slipped his hand under April's arm to silently urge her out of the house. "Maybe we'd better go."

Not knowing if she was more stunned by the information that her grandmother was indeed here, unchaperoned in the middle of the night with a man, or by Jimmy's all-too-familiar behavior toward her, April yanked her arm away from him.

"No, we'd better not. Where is she?" she demanded, her eyes pinning Yuri.

"I'm right here, April."

April swung around to see her grandmother standing in the narrow hall that led to the back of the house.

"No need to let the people in Anchorage know you're looking for me."

"Gran, how could you?"

"How could I what? Come here with a man I've known for over twenty years to share some conversation and a little of his Russian vodka? Easily." With a dignity and humor that instantly captivated Jimmy and made him the older woman's everlasting fan, Ursula Hatcher raised her chin like a queen. "Your timing's terrible, April."

"My…my timing?" April stammered incredulously. "*My* timing is terrible?" Was her grandmother out of her mind? People her age and in her condition didn't just play with fire the way she knew her grandmother intended. It was too dangerous. "You're getting ready to re-enact *Lady Chatterley's Lover,* knowing what that could do to your heart, and you're telling me *my* timing is terrible? I'd say my timing is damn good."

Ursula's expression reflected an angelic disposition—and a made-up mind. "Not that I'm dignifying your accusation with a denial, but it's my heart, April, and I get to do with it what I want."

April didn't see it that way. "A corner of that heart is mine and I want it preserved." Because she didn't want to take out her anger on her grandmother, she whirled on Yuri instead. "And you, what do you mean bringing her out here at this time of night? She's a sick woman. She belongs in bed—her own bed."

Yuri's jaw dropped as he looked from Ursula to April. "She does not behave like a sick woman." He smiled a little, looking at Ursula. "She behaves like a young girl."

Ursula beamed. "Thank you, Yuri, I *feel* like a young girl."

April's temper was dangerously close to the edge. "A young girl with a heart condition," she shouted. Annoyed at losing her temper, she turned to Jimmy, her tone less than friendly. "You're a doctor, back me up here."

Just like that, Jimmy found himself the focus of three sets of eyes, one angry, one pleading and one bewildered and confused. Like a man walking on thin ice, he took his steps carefully.

"I'd say this is pretty stressful right now." He looked at Ursula and smiled kindly. "How do you feel, Mrs. Hatcher?"

"Fine," she announced proudly, tossing her head slightly as she looked at April.

Well, of course she'd say that, April thought. She'd have to. "Don't take her word for it."

"Whose word should I take?"

Jimmy's tone grated on her nerves. She should have known better than to ask someone like him to be sensible. He probably thought this was a great joke.

"She'd be the best authority on what she's feeling, wouldn't you, Mrs. Hatcher?"

"Ursula," Ursula told him softly.

Great, now she was flirting with the doctor. "Don't you have a stethoscope or something?" April demanded.

"Not on me." A smile played along his lips. "I didn't think I'd need it for the saloon."

He did, however, take Ursula's hand in his. With two fingers on her pulse, he timed the rhythm, glancing at his watch.

"Seems fine to me, given the situation." He looked at April significantly, his eyes taking full measure of her and the way her breasts heaved with each angry breath she took. "Steadier than my own right now."

It was hopeless. She had no one to depend on but herself. What else was new? "Let's go, Gran. We're going home."

"I'll go home when I'm ready, dear," Ursula said

sweetly. Her eyes shifted toward Yuri, who was standing off to the side. "Yuri was just getting to the good part—in his story," she added with what looked to be an almost wicked smile to Jimmy. "And, as you seem to want to believe, I haven't much time left. I'd like to enjoy whatever time there is, thank you."

April opened her mouth to refute the statement, but nothing came out.

"She has a point," Jimmy commented.

She wanted to hit him. And shake some sense into her grandmother and Yuri. Instead, confounded and outnumbered, April sighed. "All right, stay. I give up." Upset, worried, she turned on her heel and walked out.

"I'll be home before morning," Ursula called after her.

About to follow April, Jimmy looked over his shoulder and winked at Ursula. "Don't overdo it. Doctor's orders."

Ursula watched the young man hurry after her granddaughter. Her smile was wide when she looked at Yuri. "I like him."

"Me, too," Yuri agreed. "But I like you better. Come—" he slipped his arm around her shoulders "—before the vodka evaporates."

"Wouldn't want that to happen." Ursula laughed softly as she allowed herself to be led back to the rear of the house.

"Hold on," Jimmy called as he hurried after April to her car.

Right now, all April wanted to do was get into the

car and drive away, leaving him stranded here. But that would be giving in to more childish instincts and it had been a long time since she'd been a child. So instead, she swung around and glared at him, her fisted hands digging into her waist.

"Just what kind of a doctor are you?" she demanded hotly.

There was something very arousing about the sight of a beautiful woman with fire in her eyes. He had to concentrate to keep his thoughts from going off on a tangent.

"The kind who respects people's wishes."

That was a cop-out and he knew it, she thought. "Even self-destructive wishes?"

He pointed out the obvious. "We don't know that for sure. For all you know, all they're doing is talking and exchanging childhood experiences." He saw the incredulous look she gave him. "And if it goes further than that, well, sex is a wonderful stimulant. It revitalizes you and makes you feel young again. Yuri might be exactly what your grandmother needs."

Was she the only one making any sense? "To do what? Kill her?"

"No." In his opinion, April was overreacting. Was she just being protective of her grandmother's health, or was there something more at play here? "That's why Shayne wanted her to go to Anchorage for tests, to see whether or not she needs further care."

"She's complained of chest pains," she reminded him.

April made an effort to rein in her temper. She was tired of being the caretaker for everyone, and yet, there was no one to take her place. Everyone was being far too blasé about it.

Damn it, she'd known this would happen if she came back to Hades.

"Look," she tried again, "where there's smoke, there's fire."

He certainly wouldn't have minded building his own fire with April, but for the time being, he kept that to himself. "Not necessarily. Sometimes the wind just carries the smoke off in a different direction."

Dumbfounded, she stared at him. "Do you like to argue?"

"Sometimes." Very carefully, he pulled her fisted hands away from her waist and slipped his thumbs in between the clenched fingers, opening them until he held her hands in his. "Look, all I'm saying is that your grandmother should be allowed to make her own choices and enjoy herself." He smiled at her. "She's old enough and she's definitely earned the right."

His smile had an unsettling effect on her. For reasons of self-preservation, April looked away from him and toward the darkened house. Was it her imagination, or was that laughter she heard coming from the rear? "I'm beginning to think she's going senile."

As far as he was concerned, Ursula Hatcher had fairly crackled with life. She certainly behaved a great deal younger than her granddaughter. "She seemed pretty lucid to me."

He would say that. "How can she be lucid, ignoring her health problems like that? Her heart is bad," April insisted. "If it wasn't, she wouldn't have asked me to come and help."

The explanation was so simple, it made him smile. "Maybe her heart's involved in another way in the request."

She stopped avoiding his eyes and looked at him. "What do you mean?"

"Maybe she just missed having you around and thought that if she told you she was sick, you'd come." He looked at her, driving his point home. "And apparently she was right."

This wasn't duplicity on her grandmother's part. Her grandmother had her pride. She didn't ask for anything. Ever. "She didn't tell me. June did."

"And who told June about her condition?"

"Gran did," April said reluctantly. "But June checked it out with Shayne," she added triumphantly as she remembered the detail. "Gran has angina."

Jimmy acquiesced. "All right, maybe she does bear watching."

April looked over his shoulder at the house. She'd go him one better. "She bears being dragged out of there and made to go home."

"Don't treat her like a child, April, she deserves better than that." He saw the surprised look on her face and found himself wanting to kiss it away. "She deserves her dignity."

April frowned, then shrugged helplessly. He made sense, she supposed.

"Maybe you're right. But I worry about her." The chip she'd been carrying on her shoulder all evening slipped off as she leaned against the car. Remembering. "She's been both mother and father to us for most of our lives—even when my mother was alive, it was

Gran who took care of everything. Gran who saw to it that we went to school, did our homework, had clean clothes to put on.'' She didn't add that she'd gradually taken over all those details, and more, feeling it her duty as the oldest to take care of her siblings. And then Gran, too, because that was just the way things were.

But he didn't need to know that. It wasn't anything she advertised.

''I'd say she more than earned a little play time, wouldn't you?''

She wanted her grandmother to be happy, but it was more complicated than just that. ''Not if it means losing her.''

What made him a good doctor, he liked to think, was his ability to see both sides. And to care about each. ''It's the quality of life that's important, April, not just the quantity. Quantity without quality is just another way of marking time.''

The remark had merit. It seemed the kind of thing a sensitive man would say. She hadn't thought the word applied to him. April looked at him now, wondering how much was real and how much was just talk for its own sake.

The moonlight made him appear even sexier than he had before, in the Salty, if that were possible. She felt that same intense pull she had earlier. The one that kept reminding her that it had been a long time since she'd felt like something more than just a photojournalist or someone's granddaughter. A long time since she'd felt like a desirable woman.

She thought his words over. Though she hated to

admit it, he was right. Gran was enjoying herself and she had every right to. She had more than earned it.

The distant sound of pleasure-filled laughter came to her and this time she smiled.

Way to go, Gran.

Maybe she should take a page out of her grandmother's book and do the same. Enjoy herself. Wasn't she overdue? What would be the harm?

She looked at Jimmy. Neither one of them would be around in a few weeks. There was nothing wrong in a harmless fling, especially if it made her feel good. And she had a feeling that Jimmy Quintano knew all the places that made a woman feel good. It might behoove her, for her own good, if she stopped treating Alison's brother as if he were the enemy.

She turned her face up to his. "So, when you were majoring in medicine and minoring in psychology, when did you have time to become a philosopher?"

What had just happened here? He could swear the woman in front of him had just gone through some sort of transformation. He could see it in her stance, detect it in her eyes. She had suddenly relaxed and in doing so, she seemed even sexier and more attractive than before. He felt himself wanting her. Badly.

He lifted a shoulder carelessly in response to her question. "Just comes naturally when you've got three siblings."

She smiled at that. "Is three the magic number? I have two."

"Sorry," he deadpanned, moving closer to her. "It has to be three."

"Three." She nodded her head, as if she was being

allowed in on a great secret. "Maybe next time," she quipped.

"Maybe."

His smile seemed to go right through her. As did the look in his eyes. She could almost feel him touching her with them. Or was that just wishful thinking?

"Feeling better?" he asked.

His voice was kind and she felt herself responding to it. She knew he was asking about the way she felt about her grandmother and she appreciated his thoughtfulness.

"I guess so." She blew out a breath, making her peace with things the way they were. "At least I know she's not lying keeled over in some ditch."

"She seemed a great deal better off than that," he noted, glancing over his shoulder toward the house. The sound of laughter floated out to him. The woman certainly did know how to enjoy herself, he mused. "And happier."

"She did seem happy, didn't she?" And that, April told herself, was the bottom line. Gran's happiness. She'd lost sight of that for a moment. April opened the car door. "C'mon, I'll drop you off at Alison's house."

He got in on his side and looked at her after buckling up. "I could be talked into a cup of coffee or a nightcap at your place."

She was sure he could. And if she asked him in, she might just want him to stay. But she knew that right now, feeling vulnerable the way she was, she would be much better off not facing that complication.

"I think I've had enough surprises for one night," she told him.

Jimmy sat back in his seat. He made it a point to never push.

"I take it Cinderella made it home from the ball." Startled, April looked up from the drawing she'd been doodling on the pad, waiting for Jimmy to arrive. The mail had been particularly light today and she found herself with much too much time on her hands. Too much time to think.

She'd been biding her time since one o'clock, pretending to not look at the clock or to wonder if Jimmy would indeed show. Part of her hadn't wanted him to, and the other part had.

Now there were only nerves to deal with instead of an internal war. There was no reason for nerves. This was nothing more than a pleasant outing. And if he was serious about wanting to see the so-called sights, the outing would practically be over before it began. No matter what Jimmy thought to the contrary, there really wasn't all that much of Hades to see.

"Gran's upstairs, sleeping," she told him, reaching for her jacket. "She came in at three. The way she was tiptoeing around, she probably thought I didn't hear her, but I did."

Jimmy waited as she put up the Closed sign and then locked the door from the outside. "So now what, she's grounded?"

April laughed shortly. "Living in Hades is being grounded enough." Out of habit, because she was accustomed to taking charge, she led the way to her car.

"You were right. She's an adult and deserves to try to be happy. I just had this horrible image of her—"

Jimmy saw no reason to steer her to the vehicle Jean-Luc had lent him. It was April's tour. He just stopped long enough to take out the picnic basket Luc and Alison had prepared for them. "Dying with a smile on her face?"

"Quite frankly, yes." Did that make her seem silly in his eyes? Not that it mattered what she looked like in his eyes, but she wondered anyway.

"There are worse ways to go, you know." He held the car door open for her then closed it when she slid inside. "When my time comes," he told her as he deposited the picnic basket on the back seat of her car, "I hope I go that way." Sliding into the front passenger side, he looked at her pointedly. "Making love to someone I was attracted to."

Their eyes locking, April felt her skin tingle.

Chapter Seven

She tried very hard to ignore the fact that she felt every one of her nerve endings stand at attention. Craning her neck, April glanced at the item he'd deposited in the back seat before getting into the vehicle. She started the car, then looked at Jimmy. "What's in the basket?"

"Food, a tablecloth, a bottle of some wine Jean-Luc said they save for special occasions. Since it warmed up a little again, he thought we might want to go on a picnic."

"Picnic?" Though it was the month that bore her name, it was still a little brisk for things like that. The unseasonable warmth could evaporate in a split second, ushering in a snowstorm. She'd seen it happen often enough. "I thought you wanted a tour of Hades."

He could tell by her tone that she wasn't completely adverse to the idea of a picnic. All she needed was a little coaxing. Coaxing was his specialty.

"Well, seeing as how Hades is part of some of the prettiest scenery in the United States, I thought a picnic somewhere might not be out of order. Besides, as you pointed out, there isn't all that much to Hades proper."

Her mouth curved in amusement. "I never thought of Hades as being remotely proper. More like a ragtag bunch of houses scattered about like so many loose marbles."

The town had built up some in the last six years, thanks in part to the money and effort sunk into it by Ike and Jean-Luc. There was more to the place than there had been before she'd left, but that still didn't change her feelings about it. "It's just someplace to leave."

He turned in his seat to study her. For a second she'd sounded a little like him. It wasn't that he wanted to leave Seattle, but there was this feeling that he was missing something, looking for something, even though his life was filled to breaking. "Did you always feel that way?"

The response that automatically rose to her lips was yes, but she stopped herself and gave the question some consideration. Her response wouldn't have been entirely true.

"No, not always." Realizing that she was getting too serious, April shrugged casually. "But that's the basic battle cry of every kid—" she hesitated, remembering that neither her two siblings, or Ike or Luc, for that matter, had ever talked about leaving Hades; they'd actually been content to remain. But they had been in the minority. "Almost every kid," she corrected herself, "who comes into puberty. There's almost a mass exodus from the state every year of all the kids who turn eighteen. That's why the government goes out of its way and pays people to stay here."

"Did you leave here at eighteen?" When she didn't answer, he took that to be a yes. "Was it just an itch to see the world or something more?"

He was getting personal again. She found herself not resenting it quite as much as last night. In the light of day, she had to admit that she rather enjoyed his curiosity about her. It was flattering—as long as she didn't allow it to go to her head. "Are you studying me?"

The smile reached his eyes, making them sparkle. "So hard now that my eyes are about to fall out."

She stopped as a deer loped across the road. "A blind surgeon, now there's a frightening thought."

Jimmy laughed, the fact that she still hadn't answered him not eluding him. "Do you always take things literally?"

Taking her foot off the brake, April gave his question some thought before answering. "Most of the time. That way there're no surprises down the road."

She didn't strike him as someone who liked things dull. "Don't you like surprises?"

April thought of the way she'd felt that long-ago morning, coming down to be with her father the way she did every morning, only to find that he wasn't there. Or anywhere. Her voice was devoid of feeling when she answered. "Not particularly. Surprises are when life catches you unaware. It's better to be prepared."

He noticed the way her jaw hardened. It was too soon to ask her about that. He knew she wouldn't answer. "But then that spoils the fun."

With effort, she shook off her mood and smiled as she spared him a look. "It's a trade-off."

He could read things in her eyes. Things he'd seen in his own when he looked into a mirror. Things that still remained in his heart. "It's hard not having any parents, isn't it?"

April stopped the car for a moment and looked at him in surprise. There wasn't anything to hit, but she didn't want to take the chance on the occasional stray animal walking across her path when she wasn't concentrating.

She'd mentioned her mother to him, but hadn't said anything about whether or not her father had been on the scene while she was growing up. It was no secret in town, of course, that Wayne Yearling had abandoned his family. Had Jimmy asked Luc about her? she wondered. It occurred to her that maybe he was perhaps a tad unduly curious for a man who was just passing through.

Taking her foot off the brake again, she kept her eyes forward. Her voice was distant when she answered. "I never said I didn't have any parents."

He'd guessed correctly, he thought. He was treading somewhere that wasn't fully healed. "Sorry, you said your grandmother raised you and I guess I just leaped to a conclusion.''

"I had parents," she told him coolly. "Still have one somewhere I think." Even saying the words cost her.

That surprised him. Family was very precious to him. There were just the four of them—five if he counted Luc—and he wouldn't have lost track of his brother and sisters, no matter what, for the world. "You don't know if he's alive or not?"

He might as well not be, she thought, unable to separate herself from the bitterness that always sharply thrust at her whenever she thought of her father. "My father left when I was eleven." She tried to shrug philosophically. "The wanderlust got the better of him."

"Wanderlust?"

Well, she'd started this, she might as well tell him the rest of it, she thought. April eased her conscience by telling herself that talking to a stranger who was passing through was tantamount to talking to no one at all.

"My father came to Hades when there was supposedly gold found in the mines." To have this make sense, she realized she had to backtrack a little. "Hades was founded by two prospectors. What they actually found was a vein of fool's gold, but they thought it was the real thing and that they'd struck the mother lode.

"They found out otherwise quickly enough. Down on their luck and out of options, the two miners decided to stay where they were. Eventually, others came, looking for that same lucky strike. The hope was that the vein of fool's gold was just a fluke and that there actually was gold in the hills. The legend persisted over the years.

"It was that legend that attracted my father and brought him here in the first place." For a moment, she was back in the past. Her voice softened at the memory. "He was a giant of a man who always looked for the quickest road to everything. He never took his time, never wanted to stay put long. I think the years he stayed here with my mother were the most he'd ever spent in one place." She tried to distance herself from the events she was recounting and couldn't quite manage it. The hurt had lessened, but somehow it had never quite gone away. "He left me an atlas—badly outdated now—and not much more when he went away." Uncomfortable, she blew out a breath. "He left my mother with three kids and a broken heart. I figure I got the better deal."

Jimmy hadn't said anything during her recitation. April glanced at him ruefully. "I don't know why I'm running off at the mouth like this. Must be your easy bedside manner."

"Must be," he agreed quietly, moved by the pain he heard in her voice. "I've got the kind of face women talk to."

Probably in an effort to get his attention, she thought. There was no denying that the man was a great deal more than just mildly attractive. "You must have heard a lot, then."

He was tempted to touch her hand, to silently communicate that he understood. That he'd felt the same loneliness she'd experienced. But he figured that she might misunderstand. "Enough to know that your mother wasn't the only one whose heart was broken."

Her eyes darted toward him, anger threatening to flare. "Meaning what?"

He knew a smoke screen when he saw one. She was using anger as a shield. "That maybe you were hurt because he left."

She shrugged, closing up right in front of him. "Didn't think about it one way or the other."

"That makes you very unique. I was pretty broken up when my parents died."

She didn't see the comparison. "That's because death is final."

"I was also angry because I felt that they'd abandoned me."

Still driving, April looked at him for a long moment. "They didn't exactly have a choice, did they?"

That was what he'd finally come to terms with. But it had taken him years to consciously reach that conclusion. Years in which he'd given Kevin more than his share of grief.

"No, but that didn't change the way I felt at the time. I was pretty young and alone, as far as I saw. You kind of think your parents have control over things and that they could have somehow forestalled dying to stay with you." The smile on his lips was rueful as he remembered. "I gave my brother a pretty hard time for a long while. I really think if it hadn't been for Kevin, I might have wound up living a completely different life than I did." There wasn't a day that didn't go by when he didn't bless his older brother in his heart. "He refused to give up on me."

She wished she'd had a Kevin in her life. Gran had been wonderful, but April had always felt guilty about needing to lean on the older woman. So she hadn't. Gran had already raised a family, it hadn't been fair to saddle her with another one. But then life, she'd come to accept, was never really fair.

"Kevin's the oldest, right?"

He nodded. "Right."

That explained it in her book. The oldest one just naturally had to assume the responsibility left behind by absent parents. You took care of the youngest ones, it was what you did if fate had placed you on the earth first. "Comes with the territory."

She'd mentioned two siblings, but hadn't given him any details and he hadn't asked Alison about her. "You're the oldest, then?"

"Guilty as charged."

That she should bring the word guilt into it intrigued him. "Do you feel guilty?"

She looked at him. How the hell had he jumped to that conclusion? Of course she didn't feel guilty. Why should she feel guilty? She'd served her time here. Which was more than her father had done. "That was just an expression."

"I know, I just thought it was rather an interesting choice of words on your part." She was clamming up, he could see it. "And you did eventually leave your brother and sister."

She resented what he was implying. "With my grandmother. It wasn't as if I was running out on them." Like her father had. "Or withdrawing." Like her mother had, she added silently.

He looked for a way to take the edge off the argument he heard brewing. "Do you know that your eyes darken to an interesting shade of blue when you get angry?"

"I'm not angry," she told him, banking down exactly that.

"And you're also very stirring."

Why did he keep doing this to her, defusing her with compliments she knew he couldn't mean, compliments that seemed to get to her anyway? "You make it hard for me to be annoyed with you."

He grinned. "Good."

She tried not to pay attention to the way his smile seemed to create beams of sunshine wherever it hit.

Only half conscious of where she was going, April drove up a winding path, selecting the most scenic place she could think of. The place where, her mother had once told her, her father had proposed. There was even a tree where they had carved their initials. Before the disillusionment came.

Bringing the vehicle to a stop near the spot, April pulled up the hand brake, then turned toward him. "I guess this is as good a spot as any."

The place she had brought him to overlooked a wide, crystal-blue river. The opposite bank was fringed with trees and there was an incredible view of the majestic mountains just beyond. Jimmy wondered if those were the same mountains that the miners had hoped were the answer to their prayers.

"As good as any?" he echoed, looking at her. Was she as completely anesthetized to what she saw because, having grown up with it, she'd taken it for granted? He got out of the car, as if drawn by a magnet, and moved toward the view. "This is absolutely magnificent."

She wouldn't have gone that far, although when she was a little girl, it had been her very favorite place. But that had been because of what it had meant to her mother and, she'd thought, to her father. She'd learned better.

With a shrug of her shoulders, she attempted to appear indifferent. "It looks like the stuff calendars are made of."

She wouldn't have brought him here if she didn't agree with him, he thought. "Yes, the kind of calendars where you want to place yourself into the picture."

"It's a good photo opportunity," the photographer in her conceded. April reached into the back seat and took out the basket. "You must have something like this back home."

Jimmy took the basket from her and followed her up the bank. "Not like this." He stopped to look around. There was still snow on the mountain peaks. The tranquillity astounded him. "The solitude is overwhelming."

"You say that like it's a good thing."

"At times." He continued to follow her. April stopped near the edge of the bank. "When you've been working in an ER for almost thirty-six hours straight and the emergencies and the people just keep on coming until it almost feels like one case blends into another, you could really do with a chunk of solitude."

That was when, whenever there was a moment to spare, he'd go up to the roof to try to be alone. But even then, the sounds of the traffic below reminded him that there was no peace to be had.

"Not me." She'd had it with the isolation and the solitude. "The noisier the better."

If noise was all it took to make her happy, it could be found in Hades, he thought. "The Salty was pretty noisy last night."

There was no denying that. But that was not the usual case. "And it took almost every citizen in Hades to create that impression. Otherwise, there's almost nothing to Hades *but* solitude." She could remember a time when solitude all but defined her life. She hadn't minded it at first, because she hadn't known any better and she'd shared it with her father. But when he left, all it did was mock her and remind her that he was gone. That he hadn't loved her enough to remain. "When I was little, we lived near the mines. There wasn't a soul for miles. Nothing but ice and silence—except when my parents were arguing." And they'd argued a great deal, she remembered. "I hated that. When I heard them, I kept hoping for some other noise to blot them out, but there wasn't any. In the cities, there's always noise to blot out the sound of raised voices."

She realized she was saying too much again, giving him far more of a view into her past than she had ever intended or was comfortable about.

April shrugged, trying to seem casual as she took the basket from him and set it on the ground between them. "Besides, there aren't many choices in Hades."

"Alison told me that there're at least seven men to every woman here."

It took her a second to realize he'd misunderstood her meaning. "Why would any woman want a man who was satisfied with living in Hades?" Raising the lid, she looked in and took out the tablecloth.

Not waiting to be asked, Jimmy took a corner of the tablecloth and helped her spread it on a bed of grass that was so brilliantly green it didn't even seem real to him. "Oh, I don't know. I'd say that any man who could make it out here was rugged and resourceful, not to mention a stable individual."

He certainly knew how to put a favorable spin on things. "Is that another term for stick-in-the-mud?"

He laughed, releasing the corners he was holding. "Is that how you see it?"

"That's how I see it."

She dusted off her hands before looking into the basket to see exactly what it contained. Jean-Luc had taken it upon himself to turn a corner of the emporium he'd bought into a lunch counter. Word had it that he liked to cook and was pretty good at it. The aroma of fried chicken greeted her, teasing her stomach.

Just as Dr. James Quintano teased her senses.

"The people who remain here are afraid to go out into the world to try their hand at it," she explained, backing up her argument. "Staying with what you know is safe."

He *knew* she didn't have anything against surprises. This was proof. "And you don't like to play it safe."

On her knees, she took out the foil-wrapped chicken and set it beside the basket. "There's no excitement in it.'' Rummaging around inside the basket, she found two plates.

He knelt beside her, so close that they could both share the same breath. ''And excitement's important to you.''

''Very important.''

She was having trouble keeping track of the conversation again. The words were meant to be a strong declaration. Instead they had emerged as a soft whisper that hovered on her lips before gaining flight. She could feel her heart beating, could feel the wind ruffling every hair on her head.

Could feel his eyes on her and his nearness as it radiated, reaching out to her.

Still on his knees, Jimmy cupped his hand along her cheek. ''We're in agreement there,'' he told her, the words drifting toward her softly.

Almost as softly as his lips when they touched hers.

She felt her body quickening, tightening in anticipation. It had been a long, long time since she'd responded this way to a man. Like an alarm poised to go off. Her hands tightened around his shoulders as she braced herself for the disappointment that was to come. His kiss couldn't continue like this, couldn't bring her the whisper of a promise as it had last night. Last night had been tinged with beer and noise and everything had been a little blurry. She had to have overestimated the power behind his kiss, romanticizing it each time she found herself thinking about it.

She hadn't overestimated it.

If anything, she'd toned it down.

Either that, or he had somehow managed to infuse

even more power, more passion, into it than he had the evening before. Breathing hard, April melded her body against his as he pulled her closer.

No doubt about it, Jimmy thought. The lady just got better.

He knew it was his unquenched desire that was coloring the picture for him, and that he wouldn't be able to get a proper perspective until after he'd made love with her, but it gave him something to look forward to.

He pulled back and looked at her. "Yes."

"Yes?" she echoed. "Yes, what?"

"Just yes," he breathed, slowly running the back of his hand along her face, his thumb along her lower lip. He could see the pulse in her throat beating fast. As fast as his own heart. "Yes to anything you might want to ask."

Definitely something to look forward to, he thought.

"What else did Jean-Luc pack in the basket?" The question sounded inane to her ear, but she was desperate for diversion. Anything to get her mind off the way she was melting inside.

"I have no idea." Definitely not anything nearly as exciting as what he'd just sampled, he added silently.

Chapter Eight

It took longer than she was happy about for her pulse to return to normal.

April gave herself a host of excuses, but there were none that actually held water. Her pulse wasn't galloping like a young colt out of the starting gate because she was worried about her grandmother, or because there hadn't been anyone in her life for a long while. The truth of the matter, pure and simple, was that she was attracted to James Quintano. Intensely attracted. Whether it was when she caught him looking at her, or when his hand brushed against her, every contact stirred something inside her. Something that, each time it was stirred, grew that much closer to bubbling over.

He probably got that a lot, she thought, women being attracted to him. She could tell by the easy way he conducted himself, by the confidence she saw in his eyes. Not smirking, or superior, just a man who knew what the score was in every situation. A man who was comfortable with himself and for whom the world held little to no mystery. If they had both been part of Hades, she would have avoided any contact with James Quintano like the plague. The last thing she needed was to get her head all muddled and her emotions tangled up by a man. She had far too much self-respect and backbone for that, yet there was no sense in taking undue chances.

But they were from two different corners of the world, meeting by chance and with a finite itinerary. That put an entirely different spin on the situation.

It made it safe.

After all, what was the harm in enjoying something she knew had no consequences attached to it? she argued with herself. Something that definitely couldn't flower or grow into something potentially hurtful? Something that couldn't whither and die long before she was ready to see it do so?

Rather than be harmful to her well-being, what she was feeling right now was a good thing. It meant she was alive and could take pleasure where she found it. And at least in this case, there was no chance of pleasure taking her hostage.

So she pressed her lips together, tossed her head so that her hair went tumbling over her shoulder in a blond shower and fixed him with a knowing smile.

"Was that the appetizer?" To show she was amused and unaffected, she busied her hands and unwrapped something she'd taken out of the basket. She had absolutely no idea what.

"Depends," Jimmy allowed slowly. He took out a stack of napkins, his eyes never leaving her face.

Her pulse still hadn't settled down to a regular beat. That annoyed her. "On what?"

Their eyes met. Waves of anticipation went through her. Her fingers pressed a little too hard against the foil, denting whatever was beneath.

"On what you want the main course to be," Jimmy told her, his voice soft, silky.

"What *I* want," she echoed. She wasn't accustomed to men who put their own needs second.

His smile widened just a shade, seeping into her. "I make it a point to never do anything a lady doesn't want me to do."

There was that supposed altruistic bent again. As if she believed it. "That's very accommodating of you."

She watched one shoulder rise in a careless, self-effacing shrug, then fall again. "I try."

Okay, let's see how far he's willing to play this. Her eyes narrowed just a little, scrutinizing him. "How hard?"

"As hard as is necessary." His eyes still on hers, he tangled one hand in her hair, curving his fingers along her face. "You know, it's a wonder that they ever let you leave Hades."

There went her heart again, beating like the drummer in a drum solo. "Why?"

Was she being coy? he wondered. She didn't strike him as the type. He realized that he wasn't exactly sure what April Yearling was thinking and that excited him. There was a thrill to the unknown, as long as you didn't let yourself get pulled in too far.

"What with the shortage of women here and you looking like a long, tall, cool drink of water on a sizzling hot day, I would have expected any one of those men in the Salty Saloon last night to have set a trap for you and run off to some inaccessible place to keep you all to themselves."

Her voice was low, breathy. And exciting. "We're not exactly that primitive here."

He noted that she'd said "we" and wondered if it was an unconscious slip or just force of habit. Did she still think of herself as part of this town? He'd been under the impression that she'd felt nothing could have been further from the truth. More mystery. He loved a mysterious woman.

"You kind of made it sound as if it was."

It was her turn to shrug. She nearly looked away, but that would have been cowardly and that was the absolute last thing she ever intended to be. "I get a little carried away sometimes, I guess."

He smiled at her, reaching into the basket again. His hand came in contact with the long, slender neck of the bottle of wine Luc had packed. "Just a little. Every place has its good points." And right now, he was looking at one of Hades's best points, Jimmy thought.

"I suppose," she allowed. She tried to remember a time when she was happy here, when she hadn't minded living in a place like Hades. That would have been before she could see what loving someone so much could do to a woman. Before her father left and her mother had fallen apart. "It's just harder to find here than in other places."

"I would have thought it wasn't all that hard to detect here." He gestured toward the river. "It's the scenery—"

"Don't let that fool you," she warned with a laugh that had no humor behind it, looking around her without seeing what he saw. "Most of the time the weather can be harsh and unforgiving. You freeze in the winter—literally—and just when you've given up hope of seeing daylight for more than just an hour a day, summer comes. Summer with its endless days, minuscule nights and mosquitoes so big you could saddle them and compete in the Kentucky Derby."

She'd been hurt here, he thought. Hurt badly. No one talked about a place in those terms unless something had happened to them there.

"I can see why you never made it as a travel agent," he quipped, trying to keep the mood light. "With all that going against it, why do some people stay?"

He wasn't asking anything she hadn't wondered about a thousand times herself. Why had they remained when her father wanted to leave? Why hadn't they gone with him? Water under the bridge, she told herself.

"They like to be challenged, I guess," she said carelessly. Then added more seriously, "Or they've never known anything else and are afraid to try something different."

He knew people like that. People who wanted to soar but were too afraid to release their hold on a perch to attempt it. They spent their lives in regret. "Better the devil you know than the devil you don't know."

April took the bottle of wine from him and began to look through the basket for a corkscrew. "Something like that."

"And you left at eighteen."

"Yes." He was good, she thought. The way he asked questions would have made her think that he was actually interested in the answers instead of just passing the time the way she knew he was. "I was going away to college—the first in my family to do so." Finding the corkscrew, she began twisting it into the cork. "Gran was so proud she could have burst. The only thing marring it for her was that I wasn't going to one of the two colleges in Anchorage." She twisted the corkscrew down to its base. "Or any of the other three that are in Alaska. I was going away to UCLA."

He gave a low whistle. "Tough school to get into." Taking the bottle from her, he gripped the handle and yanked out the cork. "I'm impressed." He paused as she took one empty glass and held it up to him to fill. "What made you choose California?"

"As far away from snow as I could get at the time." The first filled, she offered him the second glass. "And it was someplace my father always talked about going." There'd been a side trip to Seattle first, but since Jimmy was from there, she decided not to share that with him. He might make more of it than it was. Just coincidence, nothing else.

With the flat of his hand, he pushed the cork back into the bottle, then took the glass she held out to him.

He touched the rim to her glass in a silent toast. "So you went to look for him."

About to take a sip, she looked at him, her eyes narrowing again.

"No," she denied a little too firmly. "He just made it sound nice, that's all." She forced her voice to sound lighter, as if they were talking about any one of a number of things rather than something painfully close to her heart. "Someplace you couldn't get marooned no matter how hard you try."

"They have earthquakes."

She couldn't tell by Jimmy's smile if he was laughing at her, or was just amused by something he'd thought of. "Not as often as we have snowstorms," she countered. "Do you know that sometimes Hades is snowed in for over six months of the year? That the only way out of here then is by plane? The roads are completely impassable in the winter." She closed her eyes. "I can't tell you how many times we were stranded when I was growing up." The memories became too vivid. She opened her eyes again. "It was awful."

"Oh, I don't know, being stranded doesn't sound so bad." He looked at her significantly. "As long as it's with the right person."

She didn't have to be a clairvoyant to know what he was thinking. He was thinking like a man. "Spoken romantically like someone who's never gone through the horrors of cabin fever."

Taking a deep sip of his wine, he held up his hand as if under oath. "Guilty as charged." His eyes shone as he looked at her.

He was tossing back her own phrase at her. April took another sip of wine before saying, "You're having fun at my expense."

Shaking his head, he corrected her. "No, I'm just having fun."

Suddenly, for no reason, or maybe because she caught herself wanting to kiss him again, she felt her temper flaring. "Is everything a joke to you?"

"No, not everything," he replied slowly, as if giving the accusation serious consideration. "But if you don't find the humor in things, you spend your life crying." His voice grew just a shade more serious. "I've seen things when I was in the ER that have made me question what we're all doing here. The pain, the suffering…"

He let his voice trail off. "And then I bring a new life into the world and realize that there's some kind of purpose I don't understand." He raised his eyes to hers again. "So I take the smiles where I can, try not to think about the rest and definitely try to not get serious about anything except my work."

He was telling her that he didn't get serious about the women who passed through his life, she thought. Which was perfect because she didn't intend to get serious about any man who came into hers. No matter how good-looking he was or how attracted to him she might be. She was never going to allow any man to have power over her the way her mother had surrendered power to her father. Intentional or not, he'd sucked the life out of her when he'd left.

That wasn't going to happen to her. Loving a man only set you up for the inevitable dire consequences of loneliness when he left. It was best not to begin if that was the end that was waiting.

"I guess we think alike, then," she said.

"Great minds usually do," he teased.

Her body heated. She felt as if he'd physically touched her even though he hadn't budged an inch. "So what am I thinking right now?"

He slipped his hand into her hair, cupping the back of her head and tilting it ever so slightly. So that her lips were in front of him. He could feel his own excitement mounting. He couldn't remember the last time he'd felt it to this degree.

"You're wondering if I want to make love with you. The answer's yes."

There went her pulse again. Throbbing and sending echoes throughout her whole body. Humor was the only way to deal with this. Humor before he saw the extent to which he was affecting her.

"You're very good."

"I try to be," he told her just before he kissed her again.

April felt herself sinking as his lips covered hers. Sinking dangerously far into the mouth of a volcano. Fire leaped up in her veins, its flames licking at her from all directions. Consuming her.

Pulling her in closer.

Without thinking, she found herself rising to her knees, drawn by the intensity of her desire and the passion she tasted on his lips. For an insane second she considered doing just what he'd suggested. What she knew they both wanted.

To make love with each other.

Somehow, on this bank, in this place where her father had promised his heart to her mother, it seemed like a natural progression of things.

But the promise had been false.

Her father hadn't given her mother his heart the way he'd professed. All he had given her were promises that were eventually broken and even though there were no promises between her and Jimmy, other than the promise of an incredible interlude, April didn't want them to make love here, where the ghosts of heartbreak haunted anything new and fresh.

It would tarnish the moment as quickly as it happened.

Hands on his forearms, she pulled her head back. The breath that she took into her lungs was shaky.

He looked at her, surprised and more than a little disoriented. He'd lost his bearings for a moment. Kissing April had set off a volley of feelings through him, like a succession of Fourth of July firecrackers all going off one after another, the sound and sparkle growing greater and greater each time. There was an urgency throbbing through him that he rarely experienced. He knew himself very well and knew that while he could walk away from some women, this was not one of them.

There was something within him that yearned to discover what it felt like to make love with her. To have her body pulsating with excitement, moving beneath his. To feel himself quickening within her and have her legs wrapped around him as the escalating throes of ecstasy took them further and further up the summit.

He studied her face for a moment, trying to understand and failing.

"Apparently I'm not as good at mind reading as I thought."

Just for now, she wanted distance between them. Both physical and emotional. Until she could get her bearings. That they would make love almost seemed inevitable to her now. And it was something she would look forward to. But not here.

"It's too chilly here," she told him flippantly, retreating to her corner of the checkered tablecloth. She drained the remainder of her wine and set the glass aside. Tilting, it fell over onto its side, unnoticed by her.

But not by him. She seemed uneasy about something, but what? Not him, he was willing to bet. He was as unthreatening as they came. Leaning forward, he ran his fingertips along the back of her neck and watched with pleasure as she shivered in response.

"We can make our own fire."

She pulled back a little more, trying not to appear as if she did so for her own safety. Right now, she didn't trust herself around him.

"I thought you said you never did anything a lady didn't want to do."

He looked into her eyes and had his answer. She wanted it as much as he. And they would make love. Perhaps not now, but soon. He could wait.

"I don't."

She pushed the foil-wrapped piece toward him. "Chicken?"

The smile that took his lips captive was wide and

reflected the amusement in his eyes. "I wouldn't use that word."

"I meant do you want any to eat?"

He grinned. "Sure, why not?" Putting the piece of chicken on his paper plate, he pretended that it took his complete attention. "Let's see if Jean-Luc's as good a cook as he thinks he is."

"So? How did it go?" Coming into the kitchen, Alison practically pounced on her brother. She'd gone looking for him the moment she entered the house, anxious to know how the afternoon picnic had fared.

Part of her was surprised to actually find him here. Alison had half expected her lady-killer-with-a-stethoscope-brother to still be with April even though he'd left for the picnic hours ago.

He'd been back for only a short while. But long enough to acknowledge that he was hungry again. He'd started rummaging through the large walk-in refrigerator that Jean-Luc maintained when Alison walked in.

"It went," Jimmy replied glibly, letting the refrigerator door close. "You married one hell of a good cook."

"Yes, I know." She turned just as Luc entered the kitchen behind her. Slipping her arms through his, she smiled up at her husband, remembering their rocky beginning, which had all been her fault. Not a day went by that she wasn't grateful that Luc had stuck it out with her. That he hadn't thrown up his hands in frustration and annoyance and just walked away. "I also married a kind and decent man with infinite patience.''

A smile played on Jimmy's lips as he looked from his sister to his brother-in-law. "He'd have to be, to stay married to you.''

Luc glanced at the empty basket on the kitchen table. "Picnic go okay?'' he asked.

Jimmy nodded, pretending to look at the basket himself. He and April had gone on to do a little sightseeing at his insistence, and then she had begged off for the remainder of the afternoon, saying she had to get back to look in on her grandmother. She'd turned down his offer to come with her and do the same. Since he was a doctor, her refusal baffled him.

"Food was great.''

Luc slipped his arm around Alison's shoulders. "That's not quite what I asked.''

"I know.'' It wasn't like him to be cagey, not with family. Pulling up a chair, Jimmy straddled it and looked up at his sister's husband. "Luc, how much do you know about April?''

"I grew up with her.'' Luc took a chair himself. "There's not much the people of Hades don't know about each other, why?''

"Just curious.'' He didn't want to use the word "interested,'' knowing that Alison would immediately zero in on it. Since she had gotten married, she was looking to pair all of them off, him and Kevin and Lily, believing that the married state was the only state to be in. Not realizing, he mused, that it was also the best state to garner disappointment from.

"April was like Junie, she couldn't wait to leave Hades."

Jimmy thought for a moment, trying to remember who Junie was. "I thought her sister loved it here."

Luc realized his mistake. "No, not June, Junie—Juneau, Ike's sister."

Taking a seat beside him, Alison looked at her husband. "I didn't know Ike has a sister."

"Had," Luc corrected. He thought of his cousin, so young, so eager to be on her own. It had been such a waste when she died. "She left with some guy who promised her the moon, then left her when she got pregnant. Ike's daughter is actually his niece. He adopted her when Junie died."

"She died?" Jimmy echoed. "How?"

"Complications after childbirth." Luc covered Alison's hand with his own. "That's why it's so important to have medical help close by. Anyway," he interrupted his own musings, "you were asking about April. She couldn't wait to get out of here, but I think her father had a great deal to do with that. I had the impression she went looking for him."

Jimmy recalled their conversation and the expression on April's face when he had asked her about that. "She says she didn't."

"What she says and what she might have done are two different things," Luc pointed out. "When her father took off, her mother went completely to pieces. She had enough presence of mind to move back in with Ursula instead of where they were staying—a rundown shack—but after that, Rose Yearling was in her own little world. Stayed there until the day she died. Pined away, actually.

"I think April vacillated between hating her father and missing him. It kind of tore her up. Ursula did her best to make it up to her, but April was always the independent one. She was the oldest and closest to her father, so it's only natural that she'd take his leaving as a personal slam." Tilting his head, he studied his brother-in-law. "Why, are you interested?"

Jimmy could almost feel Alison's antenna go up. "What, me? No, maybe just as a doctor. She has this pain in her eyes, even when she's laughing. Like there are two things going on at the same time."

Rising from his chair, Jean-Luc laughed softly to himself. "You'll find that the people of Hades are deeper than you think."

"All except my little sister." Rising himself, Jimmy paused to rub the top of her head the way he used to when she was small.

Alison jerked her head away. "You'd be surprised, Dr. Jimmy," she told him, getting to her feet. "You'd be surprised."

The two men exchanged quizzical glances as Alison walked off without saying another word.

Chapter Nine

The sign was missing from the window. The fact registered belatedly in her brain as April drove past the front of the post office sometime later. After she'd dropped Jimmy off, she'd impulsively gone on a drive to visit the house where she'd lived when things had been happier for her family.

The house, little more than a shack really, had looked so forlorn, so sad. She couldn't make herself go in.

Served her right for thinking she could recapture a glimmer of the past.

Throwing the car into reverse rather than parking it in the garage, April slowly backed up until she was level with the post office window again. The sign was gone, all right, and there was someone inside.

She didn't have to bother to try to make out the figure to know who it was.

"Damn it, Gran, why are you trying to turn my hair white before yours?"

Blowing out a breath, April had gotten her temper under fair control by the time she'd parked the all-terrain vehicle and walked into the post office. Framing a lecture, both about her grandmother's impromptu "sleepover" last night and about her being down here this afternoon, April didn't get a chance to get the first word out as she walked in.

Ursula turned away from the desk, a wide smile on her face. "So, you like this one, don't you?"

The question halted her in her tracks and effectively turned the tables, at least for the moment. She was suddenly seventeen again, coming home from a date with some boy or other and being subjected to her grandmother's eager questions, all underlined with the basic hope that she'd fallen in love with someone and would remain in Hades. It never happened.

April frowned, tossing her worn purse on the counter. "You make him sound like a dress or a pair of shoes."

Ursula's smile grew wider, recognizing the tan, suede purse as the one she'd given her years ago. "Well, I certainly wouldn't mind wearing—"

"Gran!" Had she always been like this, or had her grandmother just gotten more spirited and lusty since April'd moved away?

Ursula patted her hair, her eyes twinkling in unabashed amusement. It was as if their roles had suddenly reversed and she was the modern granddaughter while April was the stodgy grandmother. She sincerely hoped that April wasn't stodgy. She wanted great-grandchildren and April's time to settle down had come.

"I'm not dead yet, darlin'."

April's frown deepened, even though she felt affection tugging at her heart. How could someone who was so vital ever fade from her life?

"Keep this up and you will be." She did her best to look stern. "Speaking of which, what are you doing down here and why is the post office open again? I locked up for the day."

"And I unlocked it. You can't lock up the post office in the middle of the day unless it's a national holiday or we're at war—maybe not even then," Ursula added. "You wanted to go out and I think that's wonderful, but we can't have the post office locked up like that, it's just not right."

She did her best to make Gran see reason, though part of her knew she was defeated even before she began. "Gran, I did all the mail, delivered what absolutely had to be delivered, sorted and processed the rest and—" She could see that her words were just washing over her grandmother's crisp curls. She'd done her hair since waking up, April thought. She hoped that that didn't mean that another visit from Yuri was the reason behind the sudden change in hairstyle. "There is no arguing with you, is there?"

Rising from her chair, Ursula lifted her chin proudly. "Taught you well, didn't I?"

Because her grandmother had turned away, April quickly shifted so that she was in front of the woman again. "What you taught me was not to give up—ever. Now I want you in bed, young lady."

Ursula laughed. "Funny, that's just what Yuri said to me last night." Aware that her granddaughter was rolling her eyes, Ursula sighed, thrilling at the feeling that wafted through her. If anyone had asked, she would have said she felt sixteen again. And falling in love for the first time. Or possibility the second. "Oh, April, there's nothing like it in the world."

April pressed her lips together, not quite sure whether she should be appalled or envious. At least Gran was able to enjoy relationships without qualms or inhibitions, which was far more than she could say. "I'll save us both some embarrassment and won't ask you what 'it' is."

"Love, darling." Ursula sighed dramatically. "Love."

April was happy that her grandmother was enjoying herself, she really was, but that didn't negate the fact that she was still worried about the older woman. A great deal.

"Can't you sigh about it upstairs while resting?"

Ursula bent to pick up the now empty mail pouch and waved a dismissive hand at the suggestion. "I've all of eternity to rest. I'm not content to watch life go by my window." She fixed April with a meaningful look. "Like someone."

She didn't have the patience for a go-round this afternoon, April thought. It wasn't as if this was new. "I've been all over the country, Gran," she reminded the older woman. "I wouldn't say that was exactly letting life go by."

Feeling suddenly drained, Ursula still wasn't about to concede the point. "You've been running all over the country," she corrected her granddaughter, sitting again. "There's a difference."

This was all a smoke screen, April realized, to keep her from focusing on what was going on. "Gran, let me get the doctor. You look pale."

"Of course I look pale," Ursula said with a dismissive sniff. "You don't let me go outside—" April's words suddenly replayed themselves in her head. "Doctor? You mean the one you went out with today?"

She wasn't thinking of Jimmy. It was Shayne she intended to bring back with her. Drag back if she had to. After all, he was Gran's doctor, not Jimmy. "It was a tour, Gran, don't make it sound as if it was a date."

"It was a date, April, don't make it sound as if it was nothing."

Not about to be put off, April stooped beside her grandmother until she was on the same eye level. She took the older woman's hand in hers, placing a finger against her pulse. She didn't like what she was feeling. "Your pulse is racing."

Like a queen, Ursula pulled her hand away. "I'm thinking of Yuri."

April rose to her feet, making a decision. "Okay, enough. I'm getting the doctor." And then she hesitated, torn. "Will you be all right if I go out and leave you alone for a few minutes?"

"I was all right while you went out for six years," Ursula reminded her.

No, she wasn't about to get sucked back into a discussion about that, not this time. "Sit right there," April instructed, "I'll be back as soon as I can."

With that, she spun on her heel and sailed out the front door. And ran right into Jimmy. The impact was so sudden and so hard, April lost her balance and probably would have fallen if he hadn't grabbed her by her arms and pulled her up against him to steady her.

Looking up into his eyes, she felt far from steady. It took her a beat to get her orientation back and remember why she was racing out of the post office in the first place. It gave him the opportunity to speak first.

"What's the matter?"

There was concern in his voice. April didn't think to ask him what he was doing here after she'd just seen him less than an hour ago. She could only think that she was glad he'd come.

"It's Gran—"

His lips peeled back into a grin that was tinged with admiration. "Gave you the slip again, did she?"

"No, she's—" Instead of taking the time to explain anything, April grabbed his hand and pulled Jimmy into the store.

"Hello, Mrs. Hatcher—" Jimmy began.

And then he got a good look at Gran. The woman looked as if she was on the verge of wilting and trying very hard to not show it. His light, bantering demeanor faded. Momentarily forgetting about April, he crossed to the older woman's side and took her hand in his.

His voice was gentle, kind. "Tell me what you're feeling, Mrs. Hatcher."

Ursula tossed her head proudly. "Light-headed now that you're looking at me with those big blue eyes of yours."

She was a character, all right, and he could see why April would have her hands full. He wondered if right now this was all for show, to mask how she really felt. One of the indignities of aging was knowing that you needed someone else's help to continue. It was a bitter pill for some to swallow. He sympathized, but that didn't mean he was about to back away.

"What did you feel before you looked into my eyes?" When she didn't answer, he prodded, "When you first decided you needed to sit down."

Ursula did her best to shrug off the question and its implications. "My heart's a little jumpy, but that's nothing unusual. After beating faithfully for sixty-nine years, it does that occasionally. I just wait it out." She leaned forward a little and lowered her voice. "And after last night—"

He could see it was an effort for her to maintain the bantering countenance. For dignity's sake, he came to her rescue.

"See what you can do about reining in that zest for life of yours, Mrs. Hatcher." He patted her hand gently. "You don't want to make Yuri feel guilty, do you?"

She understood what he was saying. That if anything happened to her, Yuri wouldn't forgive himself. That was part of the reason she liked Yuri so much. Because he cared about her. "No."

She needed something more than just rest. "Did Shayne give you any nitrogylcerin tablets?" He saw

Ursula wrinkle her brow as she tried to think. "Tiny round pills? You put them under your tongue when you feel an attack of angina coming on."

Her face brightened. "Oh, those things. Yeah, I have some."

"Where?" he pressed when she made no effort to elaborate.

"In the medicine cabinet upstairs." As much as she appeared to like him, it was clear she didn't like her health being the sole reason she was being fussed over. "But this'll be over in a minute."

April was already making her way to the back stairs. "It's already been a minute," she pointed out, her voice sharp to hide her concern.

She heard Jimmy saying, "It'll be over faster if you take the pill," as she raced up the narrow stairs two at a time. She also heard her grandmother giggle, "Oh, Dr. Jimmy."

Coming to the landing, April shook her head, not knowing whether to wring her grandmother's neck for being so stubborn and so blasé about her health, or to just hold on to her as if she was a precious being who would, at any second, be lost to her.

She walked into the bathroom and opened the medicine cabinet. Like every square inch of the upper floor, the small glass shelves were crammed with containers that once held pills and bandage boxes long depleted. Her grandmother hated to throw out anything in case she needed it later.

They were worlds apart, there, she thought, finally finding the small, dark amber vial of pills. Everything April owned could be tossed into two suitcases.

Holding the vial in one hand and gripping the banister with the other, April flew down the stairs.

"I've got the pills," she announced before her foot hit the ground floor. She heard the front door open before she entered the office. "We're closed," she snapped without bothering to look toward whoever was entering into the post office. She had no time to play postmistress right now.

"No, we're not," Ursula contradicted feebly. "We're just consulting. Be with you in just a minute."

"Gran, are you all right?"

Focusing her eyes, Ursula saw her grandson approaching. She immediately beamed at him, thinking how much he reminded her of his grandfather. Max had grown up to be such a fine young man.

"Of course I'm all right, dear. Or I will be once everyone backs away." She looked at April and Jimmy. "You're sucking up all my oxygen. That can't be good, right, Dr. Jimmy?"

"Ignoring heart flutters could be far worse," he told her.

Shaking a pill out of the vial April had handed him, he held it up to Ursula. With an indulgent sigh, Ursula took the pill from him and obligingly placed it under her tongue.

Since she hadn't denied the term he'd used, he figured he'd described the symptom she was experiencing pretty accurately. "How long have these flutters been going on, Mrs. Hatcher?"

"Not long," Ursula lisped, trying to keep the pill from slipping out.

"Too long," April contradicted vehemently.

Pushing a wayward lock of black hair out of his eyes, Max looked at his grandmother. This time, he wasn't about to let her get away with anything, not when it involved her health.

"About two months," Max told the man who'd been introduced to him last night as Alison's brother. "That she'll admit to," he added, looking pointedly at his grandmother. It was he and June who had bullied the older woman into going to see Shayne in the first place. But she'd staunchly refused to go for a follow-up visit, or to fly to Anchorage for any tests.

The look Ursula gave Jimmy was the last word in innocence. She lifted her shoulders helplessly, then let them drop, as if to indicate that she had no idea what her grandchildren were talking about.

"Don't let that face fool you," April warned Jimmy. "She's sick and she knows it. She also knows that it'll only get worse, but she refuses to submit to any of the tests."

The sweet smile melted into a stubborn expression. "This is my home and I don't want to leave it so a bunch of doctors I don't know and who don't know me can poke around, shake their heads and make mistakes." She looked from one grandchild to the other before sparing Jimmy a glance. "Lost my second husband that way. Mica trusted everyone and now he's gone. That's not going to happen to me."

That sounded almost like her own protest, April thought. Except in her case, she'd meant it about falling in love and suffering her mother's fate. This was a great deal more immediate—and serious at the moment. Her grandmother had to be made to see reason.

Kneeling beside her, April tried her best to be persuasive instead of impatient. "Gran, medicine's come a long way since then."

"Well, then it can come a little further and come here to me," Ursula informed her complacently. She looked at the two men standing on either side of her. "Anything's going to be done, it's going to be done right here in Hades."

"We don't have a hospital," April insisted, struggling to not raise her voice. Her grandmother could be more infuriating than a battalion of disobedient children at times.

"We have a doctor," Ursula countered. She looked pointedly at Jimmy. "Two by my count."

Jimmy shook his head. Though he saw a great deal of beauty in this wilderness his sister had chosen to remain in, he was basically a city kid at heart. "I'm only visiting."

Ursula smiled at him. "But you're here now."

Jimmy saw Ursula and April look at one another in momentary silence, each determined in her own way to move the other. If pressed, he wouldn't have known which one to bet on to win.

He tried to tilt the odds in April's favor.

"Mrs. Hatcher, they have a great deal more equipment at Providence Hospital than Shayne has available to him here. I'm sure he'd fly in with you to Anchorage and be the attending physician." Alison had mentioned that the hospital listed him as being on their staff so it should be an easy matter to perform the tests on Ursula. "That should make you feel better." He squeezed her hand. "Why don't you think about it?"

Ursula nodded. "All right, dear, I'll do just that if it makes you happy."

Ignoring her brother, hooking her arm through Jimmy's, April pulled him over to the side. "And while she's thinking about it," she rasped in his ear, "Gran could die."

"The alternative is to throw a bag over her head and kidnap her and I think the excitement of that might do a lot more harm than good." Jimmy looked over his shoulder at the older woman. All in all, she seemed to be of rugged, pioneer stock. "Although I don't know…"

Rising to her feet, Ursula pushed between them. "Don't stand there whispering about me and think I don't hear. You develop wonderful hearing in these parts. At any given time in the winter I can tell you where the snowflakes are falling," she told Jimmy proudly. "And my eyesight's pretty keen, too," she added with a chuckle.

Jimmy noted with relief that the color was returning to the older woman's cheeks. A great many patients suffering from angina needed nothing more to maintain a fine quality of life than to occasionally take nitrogylcerin tablets to steady their flutters. Ursula might be one of them, although without proper tests, he wouldn't be able to make that determination.

"Feeling better?" he asked.

"Having a handsome young man fuss over me always makes me feel better." She looked at her grandson. "That includes you, Max." Ursula shifted her attention to the young doctor at her granddaughter's side. Now there was a match she could easily approve of. "Stay for dinner, Dr. Jimmy?"

He was about to say yes when he saw the expression on April's face. He didn't want her to think he was crowding her. "No, I have to be getting back. But thank you. Maybe some other time."

"Tomorrow night?" Ursula suggested, making no effort to hide her eagerness. She tried to make the invitation more enticing. "It'll give you a chance to look in on me and see how I'm doing." Ursula cocked her head, doing her best to appeal to whatever part of him could be moved to say yes. "Don't all good doctors look in on people they've treated?"

Jimmy laughed, thoroughly enjoying her. "Taking your pulse and slipping a pill under your tongue isn't exactly treating you."

"It's the way you did it," Ursula told him with a wink.

He'd held out as long as he could. Avoiding looking at April, he took Ursula's hand in his again and kissed it. "Tomorrow night it is."

Ursula held her hand up as if she'd been touched by something special. "April will walk you to the door, won't you, April?"

April saw Max's lips twitch. He was trying not to laugh and doing a damn poor job of it in her estimation. "Gran, it's twelve steps, I'm sure he can manage by himself."

"Managing and being polite are two different things," Ursula noted pointedly.

It was easier to give in than to argue the matter. With a sigh, April nodded her head toward Jimmy and fell into step beside him as he walked to the door. Stepping outside, she closed the door behind her, half afraid Gran would begin yelling out instructions.

"I'm sorry about that."

"About what?" He glanced through the window at Ursula. The woman had moved behind the counter and was doing something. It looked as if she was ignoring Max who stood talking to her back. "I think she's charming."

"It gets a little thin after a while, but yes, I guess charming might be one word for it." She spared her grandmother a glance through the window and tried to not let affection soften her determination to do the right thing. "She likes to get what she wants."

"As long as no one's hurt, what's the harm?"

"That's just it. I'm afraid someone will be harmed—her."

"I'll see what I can do about talking her into going for those tests at dinner."

Easier said than done, April thought. She'd been at it for days and had gotten nowhere. "I'd start rehearsing now if I were you."

"Well, for that, I'll need an audience. What are you doing later on tonight?"

His smile was slow, like molasses in winter. And like molasses, it coated everything it touched. She found herself backpedaling. "Well, I—"

To hell with not seeming pushy. He didn't have all that much time here and he wanted to see her. "I'm sure Luc won't mind lending me his car. I can be here after dinner." He saw the excuse forming on her lips. "Or later if you like."

Maybe this was a bad idea, she thought. "No, really, I—"

"If I'm going to be convincing, I'm going to need to rehearse," he reminded her.

Yeah, and she had an idea just what it was he wanted to rehearse. "Something tells me you don't need to rehearse anything at all."

He grinned then. She was too smart for him to feign innocence. "Okay, then we'll think of this as a dress rehearsal—a dry run."

She doubted that, too. It would be a full-fledged performance. She could feel anticipation snapping steely bracelets around her wrists, holding her prisoner. "Why is it that when I talk to you, I get the feeling that there's a lot more being said between us than the actual words I hear?"

He brushed back the hair from her face that the wind insisted on blowing around. "It's a complex world we live in, April. Nothing is ever cut-and-dried anymore. Humphrey Bogart would have had a tough time in this world."

She blinked, slightly confused. "Humphrey Bogart?"

"Sure. *Casablanca.* A kiss is still a kiss, a sigh is still a sigh—" The look on her face told him she wasn't following. "Don't tell me you don't know the words to that classic song."

"All right, I won't."

"Luc's got a piano at his place. I'll play it for you later."

"You play piano." It wasn't a question, just an astonished statement.

"Yes."

"And perform surgery."

He held up his hands, as if examining them for the first time. His fingers were long and slender, perfect for either task. "Not such a huge leap, really."

A diplomat, a surgeon and a musician. Dr. James Quintano was beginning to sound like an old-fashioned Renaissance man—or a jack-of-all-trades. "What else do you do?"

Her mouth was tempting when she turned it up like that. He found he had to hold himself in check to keep from kissing her. "I've got more than ten days left on my vacation. Maybe we'll find out in that time."

"We'll see."

The ante has just upped itself. He loved a challenge, always had, always would.

"Yes," he promised softly. "We will."

Chapter Ten

Maybe Gran didn't need those tests after all, April thought, glancing across the table at her grandmother the following evening. Beaming, the older woman was so lit up, the northern lights would pale in comparison.

Watching her, April sipped a little red wine from her goblet. Maybe all Gran needed was to have good-looking men around to play up to. And to have them pay attention to her the way Jimmy had from the moment he'd walked in through the door and all during dinner. Having him here certainly brought out the color in her grandmother's cheeks.

As far back as April could remember, her grandmother had never acted her age. The only time Ursula had come even remotely close to her own age was when she'd laid her daughter to rest. The memory was forever locked in April's heart. Gran had looked tired and empty that day at the cemetery. But then she had rallied because she was Gran and because she had her and her siblings to take care of. Gran had never been one to indulge herself by wallowing in self-pity. The word "trouper" had been coined with her in mind.

April swished the last drop of wine in her goblet, watching it coat the sides. Right now, Gran was shining like a beacon. But then, she supposed it was hard not to react with someone like James Quintano paying attention to you. Lord knew, she'd felt it herself and she would have sworn that her heart was a veritable glacier.

Their eyes met as she reached for the bottle of wine he had brought when he had arrived. So did their fingers. April withdrew her hand as Jimmy picked up the bottle and did the honors, filling her goblet and then topping off his own.

But then, April reminded herself firmly, it wasn't her heart that was involved. Just a bunch of stray female hormones, that was all. Hormones were responsible for her reaction, including the little flip-flop of her heart just now when their fingers touched.

Taking another sip as she watched Gran shamelessly flirt with the young surgeon, April could feel herself growing warm as her thoughts insisted on drifting. Thinking of what might have happened if she hadn't backed away during the picnic. If she had sunken into that kiss and not retreated at the last moment. They would have made love.

This feeling was just physical, nothing more, she maintained adamantly. She would have to be made of iron to not have her hormones react to a man who was

so good-looking, he made your teeth ache in anticipation—never mind the rest of you.

She avoided making eye contact with her grandmother, knowing full well what she would see in the
woman's eyes. *I'm warming him up for you, April.
Don't toss this one away.*

Gran was nothing if not predictable. But April loved
her dearly, anyway.

"You seem to be, if you'll pardon the expression,
just what the doctor ordered," April said, walking
Jimmy to the door a few hours later.

Her grandmother had tactfully and strategically
withdrawn, saying something about needing her rest.
A first since April had arrived. She knew that Jimmy
had easily seen through the excuse and to April's relief, had made no comment on it.

At the very least, Alison's brother was a gentleman,
she thought, wrapping her arms around herself. It
might be spring in Alaska, but it certainly didn't feel
like spring. She missed Los Angeles with its smell of
summer in the air. Here there was the smell of snow
in the air. Snowstorms were not unheard of this time
of year. On the contrary, they were almost common.
She couldn't wait to get back to a saner climate.

The comment amused him. "Are you speaking in
the first person, or is this a reference to something I
seem to have missed?"

"Nobody could have missed the way Gran was flirting with you. That was good for her."

He laughed. The evening had been a complete pleasure for him. He'd enjoyed the company of both

women for different reasons. "She must have been really something when she was younger."

Nothing got to April faster than having her grandmother appreciated. "That she was. Turned down thirty-five proposals before she accepted my grandfather's, or so the story goes when Gran tells it. She was seventeen when she married him." Her mouth curved. "Which is why, I guess, she despairs about me."

Jimmy cocked his head, studying her face. He poked his tongue in his cheek. "And you're a spinster of about, what, twenty-two?"

Did she look that young? There were times she felt twice as old. "Twenty-five. Next month," she added after a beat.

Jimmy splayed his hand across his chest, taking a step backward as he dramatically rolled his eyes. "And you're still walking without a cane? Another miracle of modern science."

She didn't know whether to be annoyed or amused, but his smile was infectious. "Don't laugh, Gran really worries about me."

He didn't doubt it. He felt the unspoken love the minute he'd stepped into the house. "And you really worry about her. I'd say it was a trade-off."

He was comparing apples and oranges, she thought. "My concerns are legitimate."

And so, Jimmy thought, were Ursula's. At least to Ursula. "So, you're single because—what?—you never met the right man."

Just slightly miffed, April raised her chin. "I'm single because I choose to be."

He did admire a woman of spirit, Jimmy thought. "Touché."

April's eyes narrowed as she turned the tables. "How about you?"

"At the risk of sounding like I'm plagiarizing, ditto."

Suddenly loathe to have the last bit of the evening end, April found herself drawing the conversation out. "You must meet a lot of women in your line of work."

Jimmy inclined his head. His eyes, lit with amusement, met hers. "You must meet a lot of men walking out your front door."

She wasn't sure where this was going, but she was on her guard again. Life here had taught her that. "I don't live here, remember?"

He leaned against the railing, his body turned to hers. "But you did until you were eighteen."

Her mouth hardened unconsciously as she thought of her mother. "I wasn't about to fall in love and ruin the rest of my life."

He moved a little closer to her, pulled in by the sadness in her eyes. A sadness he had a feeling she was entirely unaware of. "Is that how you see love? As something that ruins your life?"

April sighed. "It did my mother's." She looked at him suspiciously, unable to read what was in his eyes. Defenses immediately fell into place. "You're laughing at me."

"No, I'm not. Really," he added when she didn't appear to believe him. "I'm commiserating."

"Meaning?"

He heard the suspicion in her voice and thought again that she must have really been hurt by what had happened between her parents. "It's the way I felt, except it was about my father."

April tried to fill in the gaps. "Your mother left your father?"

The shrug was slight. "In a manner of speaking. She died. And he just crumbled." The man had been a tower of strength, to see him lose his grip on life had been devastating. Rousing himself, Jimmy looked at the woman in front of him. "The upshot of it was that they both left me and that was when I discovered that attachments hurt."

His sentiments echoed her own. How many times had she thought the very same thing? April smiled and something within her relaxed. "We do think alike."

"Yes," Jimmy replied, framing her face with his hands. "We do." Unable to hold back any longer, Jimmy brought his mouth down to hers and kissed her.

April stopped relaxing. Her arms went up around his neck and she leaned her body into his.

If she hadn't enjoyed kissing and being kissed by him so much, she would have paid more attention to the alarms that went off inside her head. Warning her that this was not just an innocent way to pass the time. That there was real danger here.

But she was too busy trying to anchor herself to the earth while her head went madly spinning somewhere else to take heed of the signs.

Here, safe on the back porch of her grandmother's house, April surrendered herself to the fantastic feeling of his lips upon hers. To the wild, mindless sensation that darted through her veins at speeds impossible to gauge.

The excitement both pleased and surprised him. In his vast experience, the first time for anything with a woman, whether it was a kiss or making love, was usually the best. Rarely did it get better for him. By the third time he kissed a woman, there was a certain familiarity to it that took the edge off.

This was nothing if not edgy and utterly exhilarating.

It made his body yearn. Anticipation hummed through him. Before he left to go back home to Seattle, he wanted to make love with this woman. He had a feeling it would be a memorable event for him. He knew he meant to make it so for her.

Her heart felt as if it was slamming against her ribs as she haltingly pulled back. April swallowed discreetly, afraid her throat was far too dry to do anything but croak out the words if she didn't.

"I'd better be getting back before Gran starts printing up invitations to the wedding." She nodded toward the house.

Looking, Jimmy saw the woman standing at the window. Sighted, Ursula made no effort to step back. "Because I kissed you?" he asked.

"Because I let you," April corrected. She knew that Gran would make a huge deal about that. There had been men in her life on occasion, but none that Gran knew about. And certainly none that she had personally anointed the way Gran apparently had with the good doctor. "The woman is an eternal optimist."

Waving at Ursula, he accepted the excuse. He did

better without an audience, anyway. Jimmy looked at the woman who had very effectively unsettled him and made him want more of the same. "I'll see you to-morrow, then? To continue sight-seeing," he added when she didn't respond immediately.

April bit her lower lip, hesitating. She could still taste him, taste the tangy flavor that even now sent her pulse scrambling again. Okay, why not? Why not agree to see him again. This was as safe as a relation-ship could get.

"All right."

Smiling to himself, Jimmy got into his borrowed vehicle.

As he drove away, he thought, *You did more than let me kiss you, April Yearling. You almost burned a hole in my shoes. And I think you know it.*

Things arranged themselves as neatly as if they'd been placed by some unseen hand. While she wasn't exactly feeling one hundred percent better—because the woman knew that would have April returning to Los Angeles—Gran insisted that she was well enough to take a turn at running the post office in the after-noons, when business was lighter.

Which conveniently left April's afternoons free to take Jimmy sight-seeing.

It wasn't a hardship. The way he took in everything, with gusto and enthusiasm, made April see Hades in a new light. One that was admittedly less dark than before. Though it was still a great place to be from rather than to be in, she had to admit Hades had its merits, both in its beauty—which she'd never disputed—and in its simplicity and grace.

By the third afternoon, after being coaxed twice to do so by Jimmy, April had brought her camera along and began taking photographs of the places they visited. Something she'd never done before. On occasion, when he wasn't looking, she'd snap one of him.

And, in between driving and photographing, he made her smile. And he made her itch. Itch for a physical union that would gratify all the yearnings that had been echoing softly and increasingly within her from the very first moment he'd looked at her.

With the knowledge that he felt the same as she did—no strings, no commitments, no hurt feelings— the pressure of worrying about consequences lifted from her and vanished. There would be no consequences, no obligations and no reproach at the end of the idyllic time that was unfolding itself in front of her.

Because she was free to enjoy his company this way, she allowed herself to do so. It was the best of all worlds with each day being a micro-lifetime within itself. And, like a woman with a limited life expectancy, April was enjoying every shred of it.

Enjoying the way he talked to her, the way his eyes seemed to touch her intimately when he lowered his voice to share an observation or a joke. Enjoying the way his hand felt when it brushed against her face just before he kissed her.

Enjoyed him.

When he brought her home the third night, she found herself lingering on the porch again, wishing that there was somewhere they could go without attracting attention. Somewhere they could be alone to enjoy one another.

But maybe it was better this way, she decided after he left and she made her way up the darkened stairs. If they did make love, it might somehow ruin everything. Better the thrill of the promise than the disappointment of the reality.

Or so she told herself.

Bone-tired, April decided to not bother turning on any lights on the second floor but just to make her way to her room. She'd sufficiently memorized the obstacle course that comprised her grandmother's second floor so as not to walk into anything in the dark.

Besides, if she turned on any lights, that might bring Gran out and she wasn't up to playing twenty questions. Or even one.

The faint light coming from the living room only registered peripherally. Until she heard the deep voice.

"Correct me if I'm wrong—" Max's voice emerged from the recess of the worn leather sofa "—but I don't ever remember seeing you smile quite like that before."

Stifling a gasp, April stopped short. The heart that hadn't yet stopped pounding because of the kiss she'd just shared on the doorstep now leaped up to her throat before landing back where it belonged and launching itself into triple time.

Recovering, she made a beeline for the sofa and faced her brother. Damn, but he had given her a start. "What are you doing sitting here in the dark?"

"Not the dark." Max pointed to the fireplace. With

only the starlight tripping lightly inside, the crackling flames gave a soft, timeless glow to the room. "I was just sitting here, thinking."

"Is it Gran?" She turned her head toward her grandmother's room, immediately alert. "Did something happen to—"

He caught her wrist before she could dash off to check for herself. Max was accustomed to seeing a far cooler April than the one he was looking at now. This thing with Gran had really shaken her up, he thought. But then, he remembered how hard she'd taken their father's leaving. As distant as his sister tried to pretend to be, he knew differently.

"Nothing happened to Gran." His voice was authoritative, soothing. "She's happier than I've seen her in years. I just stopped by to visit and was told that my sister was out gallivanting with the new doc."

That gave certain unspoken connotations to the situation that just weren't true. "I'm not out gallivanting, Max, and he's not the new doc. He's just passing through."

Releasing her wrist, Max studied her face. She was protesting too much, he mused. "Is that why you let him make you smile that way?"

She hated it when people assumed things about her. Even if those people were her own family. "You're the sheriff of a very small town, Max, don't try to pretend you're an FBI profiler. It's not a hat that fits you well."

They'd grown up trading barbs. Hers rolled off his back. "Oh, I don't know. A sheriff has to be able to read people pretty well and fast."

Taking off her jacket, she tossed it over the back of the sofa. "Nothing is fast here."

He indicated the hand he'd held a moment earlier. "Your pulse was just so a minute ago."

She frowned at him. "That's because you were playing ghost."

The look he gave her was smug. "Couldn't have anything to do with you being glued to Jimmy's lips now, could it?"

Damn it, did everyone here spy on her? "How did you know he kissed me?"

"Good guess," he replied, satisfied with himself. It was a natural conclusion, seeing that her lips were mussed. "And if I know you, April, you weren't just meekly standing still for the kiss, you were kissing him right back. For all you were worth," he added. "You were never one to take anything placidly."

She sighed, then shrugged noncommittally. "Okay, I'm enjoying his company." Turning, she pinned her brother with a look. "No law against that, is there?"

The look he gave her was framed in innocence. "None I know of. Hey, I'm happy for you. Nice to see you finally settling down."

There he went, assuming things again. "What 'settling down'?" she demanded. "He's going back to Seattle. I'm going back to Los Angeles. This is just a shipboard romance without the ship."

A smile cracked Max's wind-tanned face. "Romance, huh?"

Exasperation pricked at her. He would pick up on that. "Figure of speech."

Max picked up his Stetson and put it on. "Seems

to me you're hiding behind a lot of figures of speech to deny what's happening."

"There's nothing happening." She knew the more she said it, the less convinced he would be, but she refused to just let this slide.

"You're happy."

"Of course I'm happy," she snapped, then caught hold of her temper. Max had always been able to bait her. They were too close in age. "I'm always happy—since I left here."

Standing, a head taller than his sister, he looked down into her eyes. Even in the firelight, he could see things in her eyes. Things he knew mirrored her soul.

"This is me you're talking to, April. You were never all that happy. You always had the weight of the world on your shoulders." He saw the anger rise up, but pressed on. They'd skirted around this a hundred times. It was time to say it out, plain. "And you always acted as if it was you they left."

"Drop it, Max."

Max looked at her pointedly. She'd let this eat at her long enough. "I will if you will."

"You brought it up."

"You carry it with you."

The last thing she needed or wanted was a lecture, even from someone she loved. "Max, why did you come here, to harass me?"

"No, I told you. To pay a visit to Gran. And you." When he smiled, his entire countenance changed. The gruff face that drove fear into the hearts of his opponents disappeared, to be replaced by one of gentleness. "And to see how things were going."

"They're going. He's going in a few days," she emphasized, "and I guess I'm going since it seems Gran's okay."

He wasn't all that convinced that Gran was all right. Or that April really wanted to leave—no matter what she said. "Why don't you stay a while longer? You're freelance, emphasis on 'free.'"

Hadn't he been paying attention? "Because I don't like it here."

He remembered other things, things she had conveniently put from her mind. "You used to. When you were a kid you used to think this was the greatest place in the whole world."

She turned from the fireplace to look at him. "Like you said, I was a kid. I didn't know any better."

He hadn't come here to argue with her. If she was leaving again soon, as she'd said, they didn't have that much time together and he'd missed his sister, bossiness and all. "So tell me about Jimmy."

The fire leaving her, a smile played on her lips. "Playing the part of the patriarch now?"

He raised a brow. "Should I be?"

"No."

The denial came far too quickly and heartily. "He's a great guy, April."

"He's okay." She realized that Max had stooped down beside her and was looking into her ear. She clamped her hand over it. "What are you doing?"

Rising again, he looked at her innocently. "Just trying to see if I can see Gran's figurines through the hole in your head."

Annoyed, April pulled back her head. "Look, I

know Gran wants me to get married and you and June want me to stay here, but it's just not going to happen. Either of it. My life isn't here."

Max thought of the letters from April he kept in the old strongbox he'd found in a deserted mine shaft when he'd gone exploring with April one summer. They had postmarks from all parts of the world. It seemed as if April never remained anywhere for long. "Seems to me that your life's a little scattered."

A defensive look came into her eyes. "My choice."

There was an edge in her voice, but he ignored it. She had to be made to see reason. "Doesn't that get a little old, living out of a suitcase?"

It did, but she wasn't about to admit it. "When it does, I'll stop."

He looked at her significantly. He wanted to believe that. "Promise?"

Max was only concerned about her. She felt guilty for getting annoyed. April crossed her heart. "And hope to die."

"No, April, not die. Live."

Rising on her toes, April brushed her lips against his cheek. "I know you mean well, little brother, but tend to your own house first. Find yourself someone and settle down if you think that's the right thing to do."

He'd been seeing someone for several months, but it hadn't worked out. As private as his sister at times, Max didn't think the matter bore mentioning now.

"First I've got to marry you off." He grinned. "It's tradition. First born, first married."

"Then, little brother—" she had to reach up to pat

his face "—I'm afraid you have a very long, singular life ahead of you." She was suddenly very tired. "Now you can stay here and stare into the fire all you want, but I'm going to bed. Don't forget to lock up when you leave."

He was already on his way toward the stairs. "I'm the sheriff, April, you're not supposed to feel you have to tell me that."

"You'll always be my little brother, that means I get to boss you around." She kissed him affectionately and left the room.

Max shook his head and went down the stairs to make his rounds one last time for the night before returning to the small building he'd appropriated when he had won the last election.

Chapter Eleven

Having time on his hands was something Jimmy wasn't accustomed to. Between his work at the hospital and his heavy social calendar, time to do nothing but kick back and listen to the wind commune with the trees was completely foreign to him.

Not that dating a bevy of women could exactly be placed under the heading of hardships, he thought, smiling to himself as he walked through the haphazardly arranged streets of Hades. But it did add a somewhat hectic flavor to his life.

He looked around, thinking of Melinda, the woman who was to have come with him on the cruise. Had she come, he had no doubts now that Melinda would have gone out of her mind up here. There definitely wasn't all that much for a woman accustomed to the excitement of a regular nightlife to do.

Funny how things arranged themselves. If Melinda had accompanied him, then he would have never gotten together with April and he knew he wouldn't have wanted to miss that for the world.

He didn't have a handle on her yet, and probably wouldn't, he mused. But he knew he liked her, liked being around her. There was an edgy, unpolished excitement to her. What there was, was genuine. There were no games, no pretenses. Honesty, he mused, was a highly underrated attribute.

For a second, as he watched a gaggle of geese cross the road as if it was solely their domain, Jimmy let his mind drift. If time permitted, he would have wanted to get to know April better. There were buttons there that he was itching to push just to see her reaction. The time they had spent together so far just told him that he'd barely scratched the surface. The prospect of getting together with her later today caused anticipation to hum through his body like a latent electrical current.

He'd be willing to bet his last dime that she was really something when she made love with a man.

Someone shouted a greeting to him. Momentarily roused, Jimmy looked up and waved before he'd actually focused on the man. It was one of the miners he'd met the second night in town. The man was right in front of the medical clinic and from where he was standing, it looked to Jimmy as if the man was propping up another man.

The next minute, both had disappeared into the clinic.

Maybe he'd stop in to pay a visit, Jimmy decided abruptly.

The next minute he was crossing the wide, uneven street.

He'd discovered that he genuinely liked the noble, somewhat harried lone doctor of Hades and surrounding parts thereof. Especially after Alison had filled him in on what Shayne Kerrigan faced in a typical day at the clinic. Accustomed to dealing with emergencies at a moment's notice, Jimmy still marveled at how Shayne could oversee the entire town's medical needs, from runny noses to embedded fish hooks to accidental gunshot wounds, with only Alison to rely on.

Granted, Alison was on her way to becoming a nurse practitioner, but even after she got her degree that was still a long way off from having another doctor to turn to when the need arose. At the hospital where he worked, there was always someone for Jimmy to turn to, always another opinion to take into consideration, another physician to consult. Here, barring the use of the telephone and the occasional connection through the Internet—weather permitting—Shayne worked alone, relying on his experience, his insight and his own knowledge of medicine to get him through.

In all honesty, Jimmy wasn't sure how he would fare himself, pitted against such odds. On the one hand, it was a supreme challenge and there was something exhilarating about that. But on the other, it was something he didn't know if he was equal to and he had to admit that he was grateful he wasn't in a position that would test his mettle.

The unusually dense press of bodies, even for the clinic, generated heat that slammed into him the instant Jimmy pushed open the door. He looked around, surprised at the number of people he saw. Every available mismatched seat was taken and there were several people sitting on the floor, several more standing and/or leaning against the wall. Many of them looked oblivious to their surroundings, staring off and into a world of their own.

Though he'd only stopped here twice before, it seemed to Jimmy that there was an unusual number of children in the waiting room, some accompanied by mothers who looked more miserable than the children appeared to be.

Nodding at a few faces that had become familiar, Jimmy made his way to the front of the office and the desk where Alison doubled as a receptionist. Shayne, she'd told him earlier, had lost another receptionist to the lure of the outer world and she was doing double duty until he found someone else willing to work long hours for not-that-much pay. He figured it would be a long time before the position was filled.

Alison wasn't there. About to ask someone where he could find her, Jimmy saw the door to the first tiny examining room open. His sister came out, looking more than a little frazzled as she hurried to her desk to grab the large appointment book.

He nodded at her, but didn't get a chance to say a word.

"Mrs. Svenson?" Reading the first uncrossed-out name on the page, Alison looked around, scanning the packed waiting room for some indication that the woman was still there.

"Here."

Jimmy turned to see an exhausted-looking blond woman of no more than twenty shuffle forward. There were deep, dark circles under her eyes, silent testimony to the battle in which she was currently and unsuccessfully engaged. As she passed him, Jimmy noticed the perspiration on her brow.

"Room One, Mrs. Svenson." Alison pointed to the room she'd just exited. "I'll be right in."

"Hi, Alison," Jimmy finally said as his sister pulled out her chair. "What's going on?"

Her shoulders slumping as she sat at the desk, Alison looked up at him. It occurred to Jimmy that he had never seen her looking quite this bedraggled before, except for perhaps the time she'd crammed for eighteen hours straight for her finals.

"We've got a heavy outbreak of flu." Alison gestured to the packed waiting room. "It's like half the town has come down with it at once."

Movement outside the window caught his eye. Looking up, Jimmy saw several more people approach the clinic. It looked as if Alison and Shayne were going to be busy well into the night.

"Need a hand?"

The door behind him opened and Shayne walked out with a patient. Talking to the man, he'd still been able to hear Jimmy's offer. "I could use two. And a functioning body in between. You don't mind?"

Shayne rallied beneath his mounting exhaustion. This was what he'd been hoping for all along, to have

Alison's brother join in and perhaps see the merits of remaining out here to doctor those who might otherwise do without.

Jimmy didn't hesitate. He knew that April wouldn't be free until an hour from now and he had nothing planned other than a walk to kill the time. This way at least he could be useful. "What do you need?"

For the first time since he'd walked into the clinic at seven-thirty this morning, Shayne smiled. "Pull up a patient and follow me."

"Mrs. Svenson's in Room One," Alison prompted.

"Otherwise known as Broom Closet One," Shayne commented under his breath to Jimmy as he showed him the way.

It wasn't an understatement, Jimmy thought as he took in the surroundings. With little more space than the curtained-off area around a gurney in a hospital's emergency room, Room One, where a coughing and generally miserable-looking Mrs. Svenson sat waiting for medical attention, looked almost too small to him to even take a deep breath.

Shayne placed a comforting hand over the woman's. "Mrs. Svenson, this is Dr. Quintano. If you don't mind, I'm a little swamped right now. He's offered to take a look at you."

The woman turned watery eyes toward Shayne, then looked at the man standing next to him. "Just do something about the chills," was all she said.

"I'm going to do my very best, Mrs. Svenson," Jimmy promised with a warmth that made the woman smile weakly in return.

Shayne withdrew. *It was going to be all right,* he thought.

April's innate curiosity refused to allow her to philosophically shrug her shoulders when Jimmy didn't appear in the post office doorway at one o'clock. He'd been turning up regularly at that time for the past four days, ready to play tourist, and she had to admit that she'd been glancing at the clock steadily for the past half hour in silent anticipation. She'd begun to look forward to the outings. To look forward to his company. Being with the man was exciting, there were no two ways about that. She'd stopped trying to tell herself that it wasn't. Knowing that he'd be leaving soon harnessed any alarms that might have already gone off by now.

She'd promised to take him to the Inuit village today and he'd told her that he was looking forward to it. He'd sounded so sincere about it, she'd believed him. But even if he'd decided not to go, he wouldn't have just not shown up without telling her.

How do you know? she demanded silently, opening up the last mail pouch and dumping the envelopes onto the table to be sorted. *He's a man, isn't he? Why should he be any different from the rest? Men promise things and forget the next minute that they ever said a word.*

As far as she was concerned, Max was the only one she could put money on as a different caste of the "usual men" mold. Only Max could be counted on to come through in a pinch—no matter what.

Jimmy had decided to stand her up.

April looked at the clock again. One-eighteen. The restlessness roaming through her had grown to almost unmanageable proportions.

Where the hell is he?

Ursula eyed her from her desk where she sat slowly sorting the last batch of in-coming mail. "Why don't you ask Alison if something's happened to him?"

April didn't even look up, trying hard to appear preoccupied with her work. "'Him'?"

Ursula laughed. "You never could play innocent, April. I always knew when you were lying. You know perfectly well I'm talking about Dr. Jimmy."

The familiar title made him seem as if he were one of them, April thought. Jimmy was no more one of them than she was.

"Go on, ask her."

Looking up this time, April snorted. "I don't care where he is."

Ursula clucked. "Like I said, I always knew." She gave her granddaughter a knowing look. "Still do."

"All right." April gave in. "Just to appease you."

"Appease yourself while you're at it," Ursula chuckled before turning her attention to what was written on the back of a postcard Irene Masterson's son had sent from Hawaii.

"You're not supposed to read the postcards, Gran," she told her as she took her jacket off the hook and pushed her arms through the sleeves.

"Not reading," Ursula replied. "Just making sure of the address."

April smiled to herself. As if Irene hadn't lived in the same place since forever.

The usual bright spring sun was absent, hiding itself behind a miniwall of clouds that threw a pall on the day.

Maybe Jimmy had decided the weather wasn't right for sight-seeing.

He still would have called, she thought.

Rounding the corner, she hurried down the block to the clinic, trying to look as if she wasn't.

The moment she opened the door, she debated turning back. It seemed silly to bother Alison about the whereabouts of her brother when the nurse so obviously had her hands full. The clinic looked as if it was filled to capacity.

But just as April was about to turn around and leave, Alison looked up. "Are you looking for Jimmy?"

So much for discretion, April thought, then nearly laughed at herself. As if anything happened in this town without everyone else knowing about it.

"Just wondering where he was," she said casually. "We were supposed to meet at one and he didn't show up." Did that sound as if she cared? she wondered. She didn't want it to.

"He's inside." Alison nodded toward the door on her left. "You might not want to hang around here too long—" A thought struck her. "Unless you're starting to feel sick, too?"

April shook her head. That would have been a novelty for her. She'd never been sick, not a single day that she could remember. Not a cold, not a bellyache, nothing. Healthiest child in Hades, her grandmother loved to brag. April hadn't seen it as much of an accomplishment. It wasn't as if she had any say in the matter. But the people in these parts, she'd felt, were easily entertained and anything the least bit out of the ordinary was news to be digested and rehashed. Over and over again.

These people desperately needed cable TV, she thought. ·

"No, I'm not sick," she assured Alison. "But I'll just slip out. You might tell Jimmy I was here when you get the chance." Not that it mattered, she added silently, about to make her getaway.

The door directly to Alison's left opened and Jimmy, following a barrel-chested miner twice his size who looked the epitome of misery, walked out.

"And don't forget to drink at least eight glasses of water a day," Jimmy was saying.

The miner looked even more miserable. "Water, huh? Ain't had water since I was a kid." A hopeful look entered the watery green eyes. "You sure it can't be whiskey, now?"

Jimmy laughed at the feeble attempt. "Not unless you want to be really dehydrated." The miner looked at him blankly in response. Jimmy smiled. Simplicity was obviously in order here. "No whiskey."

The man nodded a round, clean-shaven head and trudged out, resigned to his fate.

Turning, Jimmy's eyes met April's. He immediately looked at his watch, then realized he'd taken it off in the other room when the band had come loose. "Oh, God, April. What time is it?"

At least he looked contrite. And he'd stood her up for a very good reason. "It's after one, but I can see you're busy—"

She had no idea where the disappointment came from, only that she didn't like the feel of it as it all but smothered her. Backing away, her retreat was abruptly halted as the door behind her swung open and a young, dark-haired man of about eighteen hurried in as if being pursued.

"Where's Doc Shayne?" he asked Alison, looking frantically around the room.

Afraid of what this new problem was about, Alison rounded her desk to approach the young Inuit. She couldn't recall ever seeing him without a huge grin on his face. "What's wrong, Jack?"

"It's the village. Dr. Shayne's got to come out. Almost everyone's sick. I'm practically the only one left standing on his feet. My mother said I had to bring him before my grandfather—" Jack's voice broke and he couldn't make himself finish the sentence.

Drawn by the commotion in the front office, Shayne came out of the second examining room. One look at the doctor's face told April that he had been at this all day and was on the verge of near collapse himself. How could he stand it? she wondered. She'd heard that his first wife had had her father set him up as a partner within his own prestigious medical practice on Park Avenue in New York. Shayne had had money, time, respect and he'd turned his back on all of it to return here to practice medicine. Why? It didn't make sense to her.

"The village?" Shayne echoed. The lines around his mouth deepened. "Damn, this thing is spreading fast." He looked at his nurse. "Alison, I want you to call Max and tell him to close the school. Send the kids home and tell them to stay there. I want to try to put a lid on this as fast as possible—although it's probably like closing the barn door after the horse has escaped.''

Hands on his hips, Shayne looked around the waiting room. For each patient he treated, it seemed as if two more appeared. He didn't know how much longer he could keep up at this rate. It would have been worse if Jimmy hadn't offered his services.

Looking at the waiting room, he tried to gauge how much longer it would take him to make a dent in the crowd. ''Jack, tell your mother I'll be there as soon as I can.''

''But my grandfather needs you now.''

Shayne sighed, frustrated. No one knew just how old Jack's grandfather was, but it was the very young and the very old who were most at risk from this strain of influenza.

''I'll go,'' Jimmy volunteered. ''But I need someone to show me the way.''

''Jack'll take you,'' Shayne told him.

April bit her lower lip. Jimmy was going to need help. Well, if he could be noble, she supposed she could, too. ''I'll come.''

The relief and gratitude in Shayne's eyes were unmistakable when he looked at her.

''Are you sure? This is a highly contagious strain,'' he warned.

''I'll have a doctor with me. What can go wrong? Besides, he's going to need an extra pair of hands and I can take instruction—when necessary,'' she added just in case Jimmy got the wrong idea.

"All right, then, thank you. Both of you. Now let me get you some supplies." Shayne was already leading them back into the storage area at the rear of the single-story building just beyond the small operating room. "Thank God, I made a pickup at Anchorage on Monday." He didn't want to think about what might have happened if he hadn't.

Borrowing the all-terrain vehicle Luc had bought for Alison to celebrate their six-month anniversary, Jimmy let April drive since she was more familiar with the area. They followed Jack's weather-beaten, second-hand Jeep out of town.

Jack drove as if there were a squadron of devils after him. Jimmy thought of his own wild youth and the mishap he'd had with Kevin's first cab. After giving him a thorough dressing down about how he might have been killed, Kevin had made the best of it, never saying a word about the damage to the cab itself, or what that had cost him. That was when Jimmy had finally made up his mind to straighten up and fly right.

"Where's a kid like that get a Jeep?"

She thought of what her grandmother had told her. "Doing odd jobs any chance he gets and hanging around Shayne, waiting for him to fly to Anchorage so that he can roam around the car dealerships. According to Gran, Jack knows how to hustle, but he's a decent kid, really."

Kid. There couldn't have been that many years between them, Jimmy thought with a smile. "You know, for someone who's supposedly been out of touch with

Hades, you seem to know an awful lot of small details about the people who live here.''

She wasn't sure if he was just making a comment, or if there was something more behind the observation. Maneuvering the car through a narrow pass, she shrugged. "Gran sees fit to keep me informed whether I want her to or not. She thinks if she tells me things it'll maintain my ties to this place. She doesn't realize that my only ties to Alaska are her, Max and June.''

They'd stopped at June's place just before leaving town. April had asked her sister to look in on Gran later in the day, in case they were late returning from the village. June had told her not to worry and sent her on her way with a large box of canned goods in case the people in the village were running low on supplies and too weak to get any.

Jimmy smiled, wondering if April realized just how hard she was protesting. "I don't think they're your only ties.''

April shrugged, pretending to watch the road ahead intently. "If you're referring to my initial roots, those were transplanted long ago.''

He wasn't and she knew it, he thought. He played along a little longer. "From what I hear, you don't call any place home for long.''

She pressed her lips together, curbing her irritation. "Your point?''

He spared her a glance, then looked back at the road. Jack had picked up speed, despite the rough terrain. "Well, in order for transplanting to take, roots have to be planted.''

She didn't see it as any business of his. "They will

be, once I find the right place. Until then, there's nothing wrong with traveling around and seeing the world. Especially when I can make money while doing it." She indicated the camera she'd thought to grab out of her grandmother's vehicle before jumping into Jimmy's. "Have camera, will travel."

And he, for one, was glad she'd traveled into his life.

They hit a bump and he heard some of the bottles Alison had packed in the box in the back seat clink against one another. "Is Jack given to exaggerations?"

"Not that I know of, why?"

"I'm just wondering if Shayne packed enough of that antiviral drug." He nodded toward the box. "Jack said that the whole village was down. How many in the whole village?"

It had been a long time since she had been there herself. There had been a time when she and Max and June had all played with the children in the Inuit village. But there had been another influenza epidemic when she was thirteen, one that had wiped out two-thirds of the village and along with it, most of their friends. Remembering those days now sent a chill down her spine. Her trips to the village after that had been few and limited even before she'd left Hades.

"I don't know," she said honestly. "But I'm sure Shayne would. And he would have given you the supplies accordingly."

Unless there weren't enough to spare, Jimmy thought, grimly watching the vehicle in front of him and hoping he was wrong.

Chapter Twelve

With Jack acting as their interpreter for those in the village who had never found the time or the need to learn another language but the language of their fathers, April and Jimmy went from house to house dispensing medicine, advice and comfort.

Their first stop was Jack's house, where they found his grandfather in bed, a small, fading shadow against white sheets.

April saw concern crease Jimmy's face before he managed to mask it. The look amazed her. After all, the old fisherman was nothing to him, just another patient in what she knew had to be a long line of patients in his life, seeing as how he spent so much of his working hours in the ER.

But his gentle manner and his upbeat voice as he spoke comfortingly to both Jack's grandfather and to

Jack's mother, indicated to April just how involved Jimmy felt himself to be. He spoon-fed the antiviral medication he'd brought with him to the old man as gently as if the old fisherman was his own grandfather instead of a stranger he'd met a few minutes ago.

Leaving the old man to rest, Jimmy left a few pertinent instructions with Jack's mother, telling her to send for either him or Shayne if there was any sign of deterioration in her father's condition.

Taking the woman's hand in his own, he assured her that everything would be all right.

"You'll be up and fishing in no time," he promised the old man, peering in one last time before he and April left with Jack.

April pulled her collar up as she stepped outside the door. A few snow flurries had begun to fall.

"You realize that he hardly understood a word you were saying," she told Jimmy quietly.

He fell into step, following Jack to the next house where he was needed. "That's all right, he understood the tone. Medicine is a mixture of science and hope. I figured it doesn't cost anything to give the old man both."

Jack turned around and gave him an approving, toothy smile. Jimmy chalked it up as covering his fee.

The man was quick, he was thorough and he was kind. Everything a doctor should be, April thought, watching Jimmy work through the afternoon. She'd met her share of distant doctors, who dispensed pills and little else.

April always believed in giving everyone their due.

"You've got a nice bedside manner," she told him as they left yet another house.

Jimmy flashed a grin at her before entering the next residence. "You should only know the half of it."

She tried to ignore the implications behind the tone, tried, too, to ignore the anticipation that sprang out of nowhere and danced through her.

This wasn't the time or the place to think about things like that.

However, they refused to completely disappear.

It astounded April how easily this stranger seemed to fit in. Within moments of entering each home, after Jack took care of the initial introductions, Jimmy was welcomed into the bosom of each family like a returning long lost friend bearing gifts. He examined children, seniors long past their prime and those in between. Everyone who was either ill with the flu or coming down with it. Over and over again, she heard him repeat instructions as if he were saying them for the first time instead of for the twentieth or so. Rather than examining patients and then quickly retreating, he remained and answered questions, soothed concerns, treated other maladies than just the one that had brought him to the village. The serum and the medication Shayne had sent were in sufficient supply. No one, luckily, had to do without.

The hours slipped away as the sky above the village grew angrier looking. What April had expected to be a two-hour run at most had more than doubled in length of time. And all the while, the weather grew steadily drearier and more ominous.

Feeling wired and ready to go on for hours longer, Jimmy looked at his adolescent interpreter as he emerged from a curtained-off alcove that served as a child's bedroom. He'd finally gotten the little girl's fever down and he felt about twelve feet tall.

He paused to stretch, his back beginning to ache. "Is that the last of them?" he asked Jack.

"Yes." Jack looked far more tired than the man he was translating for.

He and April waited in silence as Jimmy stopped to talk to the little girl's parents, each of whom appeared as if they were coming down with the flu, as well.

Jimmy inoculated both of them.

"You've been to every house," Jack assured him as they walked out together. Because Jimmy was walking quickly to the car to deposit his now empty medical bag, Jack lengthened his stride to keep up. "Everyone wants me to tell you that they don't know how to thank you."

Tossing the bag inside, Jimmy swung the door closed again. The flurries were getting thicker. "That's easy," he answered the boy. "They can get well, that's thanks enough. Beyond that—" he leaned a hip against the car "—I'd sure love a cup of coffee."

Rubbing the arm that the doctor inoculated right after he'd seen his grandfather, Jack beamed. Here was a request he could grant.

"My mother will take care of that."

Jimmy turned toward April, remembering belatedly that maybe he should ask her if she preferred to hurry home. As far as he knew, there was no storm warning out, but he'd learned to be prepared for the unexpected. He saw the uneasy look on her face. Habit had him placing his hand to her forehead.

"You're not coming down with it, are you?" She shook her head, pulling away, but he wasn't satisfied. "What's the matter?"

Circling his car, she stood by the passenger side like someone waiting for something to happen. "We stayed longer than I thought we would. It's getting dark."

He looked up. Snowflakes melted against the heat of his cheeks. He glanced in her direction. "So it is. Is that a problem?"

"Not if the storm doesn't break it isn't." But she for one would feel a great deal better if they were back in Hades than out here, where shelter was a relative term at best.

"You're welcome to remain here," Jack told them, pointing toward his own house, which was in somewhat better condition than the surrounding buildings, some of which appeared to be from the beginning of the last century. "You can have my room." The young man's voice echoed of his eagerness to somehow repay Jimmy for what he had done for them.

Jimmy slanted a look toward April. He was willing, but he could see by her expression that she was not. He sensed that despite alerting her sister, April was eager to get home to her grandmother.

He turned toward Jack. "Thanks, but maybe we'd better be on our way."

Jack was determined to show his gratitude somehow. "What about the coffee?"

That tempted him, but not enough to cause further

delay. If April wanted to get back, then they were going to get back. She knew the lay of the land far better than he did.

"I'll take a rain check." He swung open his door again. "I'll be back tomorrow to check on your grandfather and a few of the others." With that, he got inside the car. April was right beside him, buckling up before he had the key in the ignition.

"You didn't have to do that, you know," April told him as they pulled away from the village.

His brows drew together as he turned on the windshield wipers. Was it his imagination, or was it coming down harder all of a sudden? "Do what?"

"Promise to come back." She frowned as she looked out the windshield. This didn't look promising. "They're not your responsibility."

He didn't quite see it that way. "Shayne looked as if he more than had his hands full at the clinic. Besides, I treat them, they become my patients."

She couldn't bank down the admiration that rose within her. "As simple as that?"

It was the only way he ever looked at it. "Why muddy it up with a lot of whereas and qualification? I'm not a lawyer."

"Just a simple country doctor?"

He heard the amusement in her voice. Squinting at the road, he didn't dare look in her direction, even though there was nothing out there for him to hit. Visibility was swiftly decreasing.

"Surgeon," Jimmy corrected. "But just because I'm a damn good one doesn't mean I have to get a God complex about it."

She didn't know whether to laugh at his terminology or to admire his obvious selfless philosophy. "I guess you're not all alike."

He didn't follow. "How's that?"

Rolling down her window for a second, she craned her neck and looked out. The weather gave no indications of letting up. She should have made him leave earlier. "I dated a doctor once."

"Oh?"

She heard the interest in his voice and wondered if it was the male of the species feeling a challenge coming on, or if he was just making conversation. "A neurosurgeon. He thought he walked on water."

He'd run into some of those along the way. He couldn't fault her apt description. "I only walk on shallow puddles."

She laughed and the sound warmed him as much as the look of gratitude on the faces of the family members of the patients he'd treated.

The window still open, the wind whipped her laughter away, dissolving it between its teeth as it began to moan. Glancing at her quickly, he saw the smile fade from her face.

"Can you make this thing go faster?"

She was worried, he thought. About her grandmother, or about them? "Probably. But I can't really make out things that easily anymore. I wouldn't want to run into a moose or whatever wildlife is out here."

"All the wildlife has found adequate shelter by now. They're usually smarter than people that way," April quipped. "Damn, it looks like that stormfront that was supposed to miss us lost its way and is coming straight for the area.''

Maybe it wasn't as bad as she made it sound. He'd been in snowstorms before and had always found them rather intriguing in their own right. ''Actually, I ordered ahead for that. It's kind of romantic, don't you think?''

Romantic again, she thought. She ignored the word and concentrated on the reality of the situation. This man just didn't have a clue about how brutal life here could be, did he? How could he? He came from a big city where if there was too much snow, the snowplows took care of it. Here help usually meant relying on your own instincts for survival.

She shook her head. ''Spoken like a man who's never been snowed in.''

He thought of the possibilities. Of having nothing to do but hold her in his arms, soft and pliant. ''That sounds romantic, too.''

She wasn't listening. Not to him. April was listening to the howl of the wind. The snow was falling harder, cutting visibility down to a few feet in front of the vehicle. ''Stop the car.''

Puzzled, Jimmy looked at her. They hadn't hit anything. ''Why?''

She hadn't expected him to question her about the order. ''Because I'm going to drive. You don't know your way around here.''

He still didn't understand. This was just retracing their steps and he'd paid attention the first time. ''Why can't you just navigate from where you're sitting?''

Shifting in her seat, she looked at him. This wasn't

about authority, this was about common sense. "This is no time to suddenly become macho."

"Suddenly?" Jimmy released his seat belt and got out of the vehicle. He raised his voice to be heard above the wind. "I thought I was being macho all along."

April might have laughed if she hadn't been so concerned.

And with good reason, she thought less than ten minutes later. The light flurries that had capriciously fallen when they'd gotten less than halfway to the Inuit village had now turned into a full-fledged storm with gusts of wind ushering in waves of snow. Visibility was cut down to only a few feet in front of them.

They needed shelter and they needed it fast.

It had gotten dark. Jimmy tried to not let his mind get carried away with possible scenarios. He knew there was nothing to be gained by letting his imagination run away with him. Especially when the woman beside him seemed to be extremely cool.

Still, he thought, it didn't exactly look promising out there. They hadn't seen another vehicle or even another life form for more than half an hour.

He couldn't remember how long it had taken them to get to the village from Hades. "I'm beginning to wish we'd stayed for that coffee," Jimmy murmured, reaching over to turn up the heat in the car. By the time they'd been finished drinking, he mused, the storm would have hit and they would have been forced to remain where they were for the night.

All things considered, that wouldn't have been too

bad. It was certainly preferable to being frozen in a snowdrift.

She was gripping the steering wheel too hard. April forced her hands to relax.

"Too late now," she told him.

He asked the question that had been nagging at him for the past fifteen minutes, as visibility decreased to only several inches in front of them. "Can we make it back?"

"No. But there's an abandoned shack close by." She didn't tell him that it had been *her* abandoned shack. That she and her family had lived there until her father had taken off. There was no point in telling him that.

Right now, it could be their only chance.

She strained her eyes, scanning the area, praying she hadn't gotten turned around. Max used to tease her that she had a better sense of direction than any bloodhound. "We passed it on the way to the village. We can stay there until the storm blows over." *Provided I can find it,* she added silently, fervently hoping for once that Max was right.

The silence between them was pregnant. Jimmy gave voice to what was haunting her. "Do you think you can find it?"

"Piece of cake," she assured him flippantly, deliberately ignoring the skittish nerves racing through her. No sense in both of them worrying.

She amazed him. They were driving in a storm that seemed intent on only growing worse with each passing minute and she appeared to be completely unfazed by it and unafraid after her initial insistence on taking the wheel. His eyes slid over her profile. The woman was absolutely magnificent. He couldn't think of anyone who would have remained this calm in the given situation. To him it looked as if they were lost. But then, he reminded himself, he didn't know the terrain the way she did.

How the hell was she going to find one lone cabin amid all this snow?

And then, he thought he saw it. Or something. Jimmy blinked once, afraid his eyes were playing tricks on him. The speck remained.

"Hey, is that it?" He pointed to what amounted to a black dot in the distance.

Pushing the wiper blades up to high, she squinted, concentrating on where he was pointing. At best it appeared to be a faint shadow, but it wasn't moving, so maybe that was it.

"It better be." Praying, she turned the vehicle in that direction.

As they approached, the snow-laden cabin looked barely able to withstand the storm. Its roof was sagging beneath the weight of the snow and its walls looked as if they were sucking in to draw themselves away from the cold. All in all it was a sorry-looking sight, but it was standing and there were four walls and right now, April thought, that was more than enough.

Home, sweet home, she thought cynically.

Pulling up the hand brake, she turned toward Jimmy and pointed to the lone box on the back seat of the car. The box of food June had packed. It hadn't been necessary at the village, but April was grateful they'd brought it along. There was no doubt in her mind that it was going to come in handy now. There was no telling how long they would be stuck out here.

"Take that with you."

It was a needless order as far as he was concerned, but he let it pass. The woman did like to take charge, he noted with a touch of amusement. Seeing as how this was her terrain and she had gotten them this far, he figured he'd let her.

The moment he got out of the vehicle, the wind fought him for possession of the box as well as his breath. Both were nearly snatched away. The ten steps to the front of the cabin were harder to negotiate than he would have ever dreamed. Careful to not lose his footing, he followed closely behind April. He heard her mutter an oath as she jiggled the doorknob.

"What's the matter?"

"The door's stuck," she shouted, the wind taking her words away.

"Here, hold this," he shouted back to her. Then, bracing himself, Jimmy rammed the door hard with his shoulder. The only thing that moved was the pain that shot through his shoulder all the way to the top of his head. "Where's John Wayne when you need him?" he muttered to himself. Taking a deep breath, he tried again. This time, the door groaned.

Or maybe that was him, he thought. Two attempts later, the door finally gave. Relieved, he took the box from her and let her enter first.

The inside of the cabin was nestled in cobwebs, dust and gloom.

"Now it won't close," April commented, frustration scratching at her as she struggled to shut the door against the wind and snow. Nothing in this house had ever worked right, she recalled bitterly.

He let the box drop to the cracked wooden floor. "Here, let me try." This, at least, should be easier, he consoled himself. Hands braced against the weathered, splintering wood, he pushed hard until the door finally creaked to a close.

Some of the remaining light outside struggled in through the windows, offering some sort of illumination. That would be gone soon, she thought, unless they could get a fire started in the fireplace. Feeling slightly overwhelmed, April looked around, trying not to allow any of the memories from her childhood back in.

It looked as if someone had moved in after they'd left and then subsequently abandoned the cabin in their wake.

It wasn't a place meant for happiness, she thought.

"Well, it's not the Hilton," she murmured.

"Right now, it's better than the Hilton." Jimmy rubbed his hands together, trying to chase away the cold. "It's here," he explained when she looked at him quizzically. "Think it'll last long?"

"The cabin or the storm?"

He laughed at that. "The storm."

"I have no idea," she told him honestly. "These things can blow over quickly, or last for days." And it was the latter she worried about.

He moved the cardboard box over against the wall. Its sides were now damp and soggy. "Good thing your sister gave us this box of food."

He seemed bent on concentrating on the positive. Was that for her benefit, or did he really view life that way? "Is that all you can say?"

"No." Coming to her, he slipped his arms around her waist. "Looks like I've finally got you alone."

She looked up at him, amazed at his composure. "You're not worried."

Jimmy cocked his head, a smile playing on his lips. He liked the way she felt against him. Liked the smell of her hair and skin, fresh and alive with color. "About?"

Her eyes widened. "The storm."

Storms blew over. He was more interested in what could potentially go on inside the cabin while they waited than what was happening outside of it. "The storm can take care of itself. It doesn't need me to worry about it."

"I mean about being marooned out here."

He shrugged slightly. "I figure someone will find us eventually."

"Maybe not until it's too late."

"No sense in worrying about that now." He nuzzled her neck, pressing a kiss there. He felt her shiver against him. "Is there?"

"No." She tried not to sigh. "I suppose not."

Releasing her, he stepped back, then stooped over the box. He read the different labels in the fading light. "Okay, what's your pleasure?" he said, moving to stand in front of her again. "Soup? Or beans?"

"First you need a fire."

He looked at her significantly and brushed the hair

from her cheek. She felt his smile reach down clear to her bones, warming her.

"Oh, you mean in the fireplace." Jimmy glanced at the empty place beside the hearth where firewood had clearly once been stacked. "There doesn't seem to be anything to use."

Pulling away from him, she picked up a rickety chair and handed it to him. "Yes, there is."

Taking the chair from her, he debated about the best way to break it up. He needn't have bothered. As he tested the back, it gave way in his hands, splintering. "I guess where there's a will, there's a way."

"If you don't stop sounding so cheerful, I may be forced to kill you." She had to admit that it was difficult to remain annoyed with him. He had such a way of putting a positive spin on everything. "Aren't you the least bit worried or upset?"

"Not really. A lot of people know where we were. Someone is bound to come looking for us and find us eventually."

That all depended on where they looked and how quickly they did it. With the storm raging, no one was going to be able to find them and who knew how long it would take? Though she wasn't about to go to pieces, it perturbed her that Jimmy wasn't more concerned about their situation.

"There could be a lot of days in 'eventually,'" she pointed out.

"Well, then, I really wish I'd had that cup of coffee before we left." Dropping the pieces of the chair into the fireplace, he looked at her. "Satisfied?"

"Guess it'll have to do." Leaving him to work on

building the fire, April looked around the rest of the cabin. She seemed to remember there being more furniture than this. Whoever had lived here after they'd left had taken everything with him. There was next to nothing except for the now broken chair and a table that listed unevenly on a floor that was far from level.

Squinting, she noticed something in the corner she didn't recall being here when her family had occupied the cabin. Moving closer, she saw it was a small, rusting cylindrical contraption.

As she circled it slowly, her foot came in contact with something on the floor. She bent to examine it and discovered a jar filled with a deep amber, almost-brown liquid. Unscrewing the top, she sniffed gingerly. The scent was strong enough to make her eyes water.

"No coffee," she told him, holding the jar aloft. "But whoever once lived here made his own moonshine."

Tiny flames had begun to lick their way around the dissembled chair. Feeling a sense of triumph, Jimmy glanced quizzically over his shoulder at her. "Moonshine?"

She nodded, crossing to him so he could see for himself. She offered him the jar. "Homemade whiskey. Or a reasonable facsimile thereof."

Taking the jar from her, he set it down away from the fire. No sense in taking chances. "Food, beverages and a beautiful woman. Looks like the makings of a perfect date to me."

She shook her head, amused despite herself. "Not

many people would call being marooned in a dilapidated cabin a date.''

''I'm not many people,'' he told her.

That he wasn't. April didn't know whether to laugh at him or to despair because he didn't understand the gravity of the situation.

She did neither.

Because the next moment, he was kissing her.

Chapter Thirteen

This was crazy.

The thought vibrated through her head.

The situation they found themselves in was so tenuous. There was so much to think about, so many plans to make. She should be checking to see if the windows were secure enough to withstand the storm, not letting herself be cast adrift on this flaming island that Jimmy and his lethal mouth had suddenly created.

But for the life of her, she couldn't summon a single drop of energy to do anything but kiss him back. There was no inclination within her to do anything but let this feeling take her a million miles beyond where she was physically standing.

April pressed her heating body against his and reveled in the hard planes she felt.

The man was a rock, a sculpted rock, and she

longed to run her hands across every single angle, every single plane.

This time, there were no hidden reasons to pull away because she felt herself weakening in a place where her father had made vows to her mother he was destined to break. There was no one to suddenly intrude on them as innocently Gran had the other day. There was no one to save her from him.

Or from herself.

Here, in the place where she had once been happy.

She didn't want saving. She would have shot anyone who tried.

Her heart hammering wildly, April could feel every single pulse point throbbing throughout her body, felt every hair stand on end in anticipation. She moaned as desire took a firmer hold.

The kiss deepened. She continued to spiral out into space, her fingers digging into his shoulders. She wanted this to go on forever.

Tongues of fire licked at her as she felt his hands caress her body. Gentle, capable, skillful surgeon's hands moving along her body as if she were something fragile.

Precious. Something he had wanted to hold and touch for so long.

The beat of her heart sped up even more, leaving her in awe. She'd never thought she was capable of feeling this way. Of feeling so much.

He'd had women who'd been more experienced, women who'd been more eager, but somehow Jimmy was certain he'd never had one who'd been sweeter. Never had one he'd wanted more than this woman, who was both strong and vulnerable, capable and needy, all at the same time. This woman who'd suffered the same wounds as he and traveled on a path so similar to his own. A path that kept her several miles ahead of love so that ultimate heartbreak wouldn't find her.

Wasn't that a heartbreak of a kind in and of itself?

He didn't know. There were no answers occurring to him. All Jimmy could think about was making love to this woman with whom fate and inclement weather had conspired to maroon him. He wanted to make love with her. Slowly, quickly, every way possible until there was nothing left of either one of them and they were in danger of meeting their end by burning rather than freezing.

He couldn't get enough of her, not her smell, not her taste, not the feel of her. The more he had, the more he wanted. He could feel the need vibrating within his very body.

The glow of the fire cast warm shadows of their bodies on the wall as he slid the clothes from her.

Not to be outdone, April mimicked him movement for movement. Buttons were separated from holes across chests that tightened in anticipation, allowing shallow breaths to come and depart. Shirts were slowly slid off desire-slicked shoulders as the momentum increased. Kisses were pressed to dampening throats, heaving breasts, quivering bellies, causing pulses to leap and breaths to grow even more shallow. So shallow that they both became dizzy.

April felt herself tremble inside as his mouth

anointed her breasts a second after he undid the clasp at her back and her bra sighed away from her body.

She shivered only a second before the fire consumed her.

Payback came when she flicked her tongue across his own tightened nipples. The moan she heard satisfied her that she had at least managed to drive small shafts of desire through him, the way he had driven huge ones through her.

The rest of the clothing vanished quickly away from their bodies, being tossed aside in haste as the heat of the moment threatened to completely swallow them up.

Get control of yourself, Jimmy chided silently, struggling to think. He didn't want this to be just another pleasurable evening for April. He wanted it to be different. Memorable. He wanted her to think of him and smile as she remembered this night above all others. The way he would of her.

With effort, he reined himself in and began a systematic conquest of a terrain that was unquestionably already his.

Nude, they sank to their knees in front of the fire, upon the tanned hide of a bear that had not drawn breath for close to a century. The still soft fur hardly registered with April. Every fiber of her being was focused on Jimmy.

He was playing her body as if it was his own personal violin, making it sing each time he passed his hand over it. Make her want to weep with a kind of joy she couldn't begin to understand.

It became a blur, a wondrous blur, with movements, all blending into one another.

She could feel her body priming, her very core yearning for the fulfillment final lovemaking rendered.

Mouths sealed, slanting over and over again, their limbs tangled as they tumbled to the floor, the points of contact sending shards of pure pleasure and sweet agony through each of them.

She'd never felt this free of spirit, this devoid of thought and the burdens that came with it, before. Eagerly, April pressed her mouth to his, drinking deeply of every sensation, every taste. Wanting more, much more. Wanting him.

Wanting love.

Love*making,* love*making,* she insisted silently, frantically racing her hands over his body. She wanted lovemaking, not love. Never love.

Lightning in a bottle, that was what she was, he realized in wonder. Something to cherish in awed disbelief. Her verve, her enthusiasm, fired his own, sending it coursing through his veins until he was convinced that they would outblaze the flames that burned so brightly within the confines of the hearth.

"Going out in a blaze of glory" took on new meaning for Jimmy.

Always before, he could detach himself. A part of him could stand back and witness what was unfolding around him. But this time there was no separation, no space, however tiny, between him and what was happening. He was right there in the middle, involved. Absorbing it all and reveling in it.

He couldn't find that tiny space, that makeshift wall

to hide behind, and very quickly he ceased looking. He was too consumed.

Feasting on her, marking her limbs with his kisses, with his desire, making her his own, Jimmy knew he couldn't hold himself in check any longer. Her body was fairly vibrating with needs, needs that echoed his own.

Searching again for her lips, he pulled himself up, slowly dragging his body along hers, feeling her body tighten, bracing. Feeling his own body pulse.

April opened for him. With a muffled cry of surrender, he drove himself into her.

Lacing his fingers through hers, he tasted her moan in his mouth. The sound ricocheted within his, joining the plaintive groan of anticipation born within his core.

He'd meant to take this last step slowly, as well, but it was completely out of his hands. Passions greater than his resolve took over, driving his body as the last leg of the journey they had been preordained to take together began.

His hips fitted against hers, Jimmy increased the tempo faster and faster until it swept them both up in its grip. He could feel her heart pounding beneath his chest as she matched his every motion.

He felt every single one of her fingernails rake across his back at the final moment.

The climax left them both spent, their skin as damp as if they had both just been caught by an unexpected summer downpour.

Somehow managing to raise himself up on his elbows, Jimmy focused on her face.

Her makeup was completely gone, erased by the

sweat of their passion, her hair plastered against her forehead, her lips an undefined blur, mussed from the imprint of his.

He thought she was the most beautiful woman he had ever seen.

Taking a deep breath, he managed to say one word. "Wow."

Her smile slowly moved over her lips until it finally reached her eyes where it settled in. "My sentiments exactly." It almost hurt to breathe, she thought. She certainly couldn't turn her head. "Is the cabin still standing?"

Jimmy pretended to look around, although for the life of him he couldn't see anything but her. She seemed to fill his very head. What was that all about?

"Just barely." Looking into her eyes, he combed his fingers through her hair. A sweetness poured itself through his veins. "You really were something."

"Ditto." She moved slightly beneath him and felt sharp licks of desire slice through her again. How was that possible? He'd just exhausted her every fiber. Could she actually want to make love again so soon? She had to be hallucinating. Lack of oxygen did that to you, she recalled. "Are you hungry yet?"

"Yes." Leaning down, he nipped at her mouth, running his tongue gently across her lower lip.

She could feel her core quickening again. This wasn't a hallucination, this was real. "I meant, for food."

"I didn't."

With a laugh, she laced her arms around his neck and brought her mouth to his.

* * *

Frustration jabbed at Max as he stood at the window, staring out into the storm that had swooped down on all of them so suddenly. April and Jimmy were hours overdue.

He'd never felt so helpless before.

"You can't go out in this storm," he heard Luc say from behind him. "There's nothing to be gained by you getting lost, as well."

As well. Turning around, Max saw Luc tighten his arm around Alison. He'd braved the storm and come to their house to see if perhaps April had decided to stop here for the night rather than continue on to their grandmother's place. June had called him just before the lines went down to say April hadn't returned.

Max saw tears shimmering in Alison's eyes. He didn't have to guess what she was thinking. Exactly the same thing that was haunting him.

"Your brother's all right, Alison," he told her with a confidence he didn't feel but had gotten accomplished at projecting. It was all part of the job. But the job had never felt as personal as it did right at this minute. "April would have found shelter long before the brunt of the storm hit them. She's not a tenderfoot."

Alison knew Max only meant well, but his assurances didn't assuage her fears. "Your sister's been away from this region for so long."

Moving away from the window and the constant reminder of the savage weather outside, Max hooked his thumbs into his belt. "It's not something you forget. April knows this terrain like the back of her hand.''

She offered a small smile at the kind words. ''How about if there's snow on that hand?''

Max shook his head. ''Doesn't matter.'' If the storm had hit up north first, April would have had more sense than to venture out in it. ''For all we know, they're still back at the Inuit village, having a hearty supper right now. There's no way they can get word to us. The lines are down,'' he reminded her.

Max was trying to convince himself as well as Alison, Luc thought. He appreciated the situation, knowing how he would have felt if Alison or Ike were out in this storm. ''I'm sure you're right.''

Nonetheless, Luc added silently, at first light, storm or no storm, he intended to form a search party with Max and some of the others to find the pair.

Her neck hurt.

April opened her eyes slowly. Why did her neck feel so stiff?

The next moment, she had her answer. She'd fallen asleep using Jimmy's arm as her pillow.

They were both on the floor, curled up in front of the fire, a moth-eaten blanket serving as a cover. The multicolored blanket had been kicked aside sometime during the night, probably only a short while ago. Otherwise, Jimmy would have grown cold and reached for it, she thought. Lying where it was, bunched at his hip, it allowed her a perfect view of the man sleeping next to her.

Ignoring the crick in her neck, April lifted herself

up onto her elbow so that she could see him more clearly. The fire was dying, but daylight was slowly pushing its way into the cabin as the chill began to settle in.

The man was magnificent.

His body, even in sleep, was taut and hard. An itch at the center of her palm tempted her to pass her hand over the sculpted form. April refrained, afraid of waking him. Content, for the moment, to just look.

She could feel her body begin to heat, could feel that same, strong urge she'd dealt with all last night take over. It made her want to run even though running was not an option.

It made her want to stay.

"It's not polite to stare, you know."

Startled, she nearly jumped. April looked up to discover that Jimmy was awake and watching her, an amused grin lighting his face.

Something within her breast quickened.

She felt a blush taking hold, traveling up her neck. "I wasn't staring, I was…"

He arched a brow, his amusement growing as he watched the blush advance up her neck to her cheeks. "Admiring?" he suggested.

April cleared her throat. "Wondering why you weren't cold."

"Actually, I was." The chill he felt, despite his proximity to the fireplace, had woken him. "Want to warm me up?"

They'd made love a total of four times last night. She found his stamina overwhelming. "Aren't you tired yet?"

The look he gave her was pure innocence. "I rested up."

She looked toward the box of canned goods. They never had gotten around to opening any of them. "You need to eat."

He caught her hand as she began to rise, bringing it to him. "Later."

Jimmy pressed a kiss to the palm of her hand. How was it possible that he wanted her now more than he had when they'd made love for the first time? That each time only whetted his appetite more? He heard alarms go off within his head, but tried to not pay any attention to them. There would be time enough later, when they got back, to get his life on an even keel again.

He smiled into her eyes. "Right now, I need a pick-me-up."

"That's what I just said." This time, she made no attempt to get up.

"No," he laughed, pulling her to him until she was cradled within the hollow of his arm, "you didn't."

Any inclination that she might have had, however faint, to dispute the matter disappeared the second before he kissed her.

April used the flat of her hand to wipe away some of the grime that had accumulated on the window and looked out. It had taken them a long while before they'd finally gotten around to getting dressed again. She'd prepared them a breakfast of beans and dried fruit, recalling other breakfasts she'd made here just like this one, for Max and June while their mother had sat by the window, looking forlornly out. Waiting for a man who never came.

She banished the thought from her mind as she renewed a vow never to allow that to happen to her. Never to let her heart be cleaved in two because of a man. You enjoy them and then you leave them. Before they leave you. "I think it's finally letting up."

Jimmy came up behind her, wrapping his arms around her waist and holding her against him. The back of her head nestled against his chest. It amazed him how much he enjoyed the way she fit against him.

"I'm not sure if I'm entirely happy about that," he confessed. "This is the longest I've ever relaxed in the last ten years."

April twisted around in his arms and looked up at him, amusement mixing with disbelief. "Relaxed? If this is how you relax, I'd hate to see what you're like when you're going full-steam ahead."

He laughed, then nuzzled her neck before kissing it. "You might enjoy it."

There they went again, those tiny sensations, skittering all along her body. There was nothing wrong with that, she told herself, as long as she kept things in perspective.

And didn't lose her head.

Her eyes crinkled. "I might at that."

His arms tightened around her, bringing her closer to him. Arousing him as he recalled the way she felt beneath him last night and in the wee hours of the morning. Like shimmering quicksilver.

"You know, I was kind of looking forward to them finding our nude bodies, frozen together in a clinch."

"No, you weren't," she contradicted. Romantic or not, that was far too drastic an end to contemplate for someone with as much life as Jimmy had. "Besides, we wouldn't have died in here."

Very slowly, with his hands on either side of her waist, he began to move his fingers in gentle, hypnotic circles. "Oh?"

It was difficult to keep to her train of thought, or to hang on to her resolve to not let this game between them go too far. "I wouldn't have let us. Once the storm lets up, I intend to get us home."

There was this spark of determination in her eyes that mesmerized him. "On foot?"

Why would he say that? They hadn't gotten here on foot. "No, in the car."

He smiled. She'd overlooked an obvious point. It was nice to know that he came in handy for something. "Not with a dead battery. At these temperatures, it's probably frozen."

April cursed mentally. She'd forgotten about that. Small wonder. He'd driven almost every logical thought out of her head. And he was doing it again now. Because she was trying to pull her thoughts together, she caught both his hands in hers and held them still against her.

"Well, in any case, once the snow lets up, Max and the others will come looking for us."

That was what he'd been thinking all along. But until they came, he had an excellent way for them to pass the time of day. He brushed her hair away from her neck, pressing a kiss there. "Spoilsports."

It took effort to keep her eyes from fluttering shut.

"You still don't get the severity of the situation, do you?"

She felt his smile against her skin. "I'm too busy sampling your neck."

She pulled her head back. "Jimmy, I'm serious. People die out here."

The playful expression abated from his face for a moment as he looked at her. "People die everywhere. I should know. I deal with it all the time." The smile returned, the one that felt so intimate, as if he'd never smiled at anyone but her that way. "That's why it's so important to enjoy life while you have it. Now, if you don't mind, I was busy."

She could feel his body against hers as he pulled her back into his arms. There was no question that he wanted her. April didn't attempt to squelch the smile that came to her lips. "Again?"

"No," he contradicted. "Still."

April felt a giggle bubbling up within her. Breakfast, she decided, could wait. This urgency that suddenly came over her, couldn't. Telling herself that there was no harm in this, in enjoying a fleeting romance that neither of them took seriously, she wrapped her arms around his neck and plunged back into the haven of his kiss.

Chapter Fourteen

Max stopped short as he saw Shayne reach for his jacket. "You can't come with us, Shayne, you're needed here."

After raging for more than a day and a half, the storm had finally lessened and Max had gathered together the people he needed to form a search party. He'd only swung by the clinic to pick up smelling salts and bandages in case they proved to be necessary, not to take the other man with him.

Shayne wasn't about to be argued out of joining the search party. "April and Jimmy went in my place. If I'd gone, we wouldn't be looking for them."

Max pushed his black Stetson back on his head with his thumb, his blue eyes sympathetic and intent on Shayne. "No, if you'd gone, we'd be looking for you now. C'mon, Shayne, be reasonable."

"I am being reasonable." He checked the inside of his medical bag, then snapped it closed. "When we find them—" he'd nearly said *if,* but stopped himself at the last moment, acutely aware that they were talking not just about two missing people, but Max's sister, as well "—they might both be in need of medical attention beyond your limited range." He looked at Max significantly. "You're not talking me out of this."

Max had always known how to choose his battles. "No, 1 guess not, and I'm wasting time trying. Let's go."

But just as they were about to walk out, the clinic door swung open. June, her cheeks flushed, looked relieved to have found them still in town. "Good, you're still here. I had a feeling you'd stop here," she told Max as she closed the door behind her. "I'm coming with you."

Max frowned. He had one sister already out there, he didn't want to have to go looking for another. ".I don't have time to argue."

"Fine, then don't." There was no way she was going to sit on her hands, waiting. Now that there was a break in the storm, she wanted to get going. There was no telling how fast the next front would move in. "The more people on this search party, the better. You always said that."

"But not to you." He knew it was useless to try to make her change her mind and if the next storm hit, they'd lose precious daylight. "All right, we'll split up. Shayne, while the weather's with us, I want to use your plane. If April and Jimmy are in an open area, we'll be able to cover more ground with your plane and spot them that way.''

Shayne nodded. That was just what he'd been thinking. "You got it."

Stepping outside, Max looked around at the faces of the men Jean-Luc had gathered together.

"Okay, we'll meet back here at dark. The first sign of the storm hitting, I want everyone back in town. I don't want any heroes and I sure as hell don't want to have to go looking for anyone else, understood?" Heads bobbed in silent agreement. "Keep in contact with each other at all times. I don't know when the next front's going to hit us but we've got an open window now and we need to make the most of it."

A murmur of voices met his instructions as the men began breaking up into groups of three and four. After one more warning to head back into town at the first sign of the storm worsening, Max took off with Shayne and Ike.

Jimmy had no idea he could feel this way about someone. The chase was over and for him, it had always been all about the chase. That was where the thrill came in. Pursuing the unknown, the unattainable. Once the chase was concluded, he'd savor the rewards, but there was never the same exhilaration attached to that as there had been to the pursuit that had been involved.

This time, it was different.

This time, perhaps because he knew that it was all temporary, the thrill was still there, not just within the chase, but within the victory.

Not only did the thrill remain when he made love with her, but it seemed to be even stronger than before.

It was as if since he knew what was in store for him, he wanted it with an ever-increasing rather than decreasing desire. And when he wasn't making love with her, he was thinking about making love with her. They'd been in the cabin for a little more than a day, had spent two nights in it and he'd lost track of how many times he'd made love to her in that time.

All he knew was that it was getting better and that his pulse raced just thinking about her.

Making love with April hadn't been nearly enough and each time they did, he got no closer to being sated than the last time. If anything, his appetite only grew larger.

It worried him a little, waking up this morning with this yearning for her, this feeling of bewildered loss when he hadn't found her next to him, but he'd told himself that maybe it was more than the woman he found appealing. It was the fantasy-like quality of the situation that made him feel this way.

After all, how many men dreamed of being snowed in with a desirable woman? He knew they were going to be rescued. It was just a matter of time. By now, they'd been missed and there were probably people out looking for them right at this moment. He was sure of it. Even if the woman he was with wasn't the sheriff's sister, he had absolute faith in his sister and Luc. They would have organized a search party to go out the moment the storm let up at little.

Until then, they had shelter, food, and each other. Jimmy was determined to enjoy himself and to make the most of the situation he found himself in, always remembering that it was only that. An idyllic time and nothing more.

Propping himself up on one elbow, he watched as April sat by the fire, combing her hair. Last night they'd fed the table into the flames. It was still burning. He noted the impatient frown that came to her lips as she tried to pull the comb through.

"Your hair's beautiful."

She hadn't thought he was awake yet. "My hair," she corrected, "is a hopelessly tangled mess. June's the one with the beautiful hair."

Leaning over, he touched the ends, sifting them through his fingers. "Not from where I'm sitting."

As much as she tried to resist, she could feel it happening. She could feel herself falling for Jimmy. Falling for a man who never seemed at a loss for words, who always knew exactly what to say. A man who could make her feel special just by looking at her.

This had to have been how her mother had felt. As though the world began and ended around one being.

She tugged at the comb again, gritting her teeth against the pain. Maybe it was just because they were snowed in.

Very gently, he took the comb from her hand and set it aside. Slipping his fingers along her cheek, he turned her face up to his and kissed her.

She stopped thinking about the comb and excuses.

Wrapping her arms around herself, she stepped out of the cabin. Jimmy had gone out a few minutes earlier to see if he could do anything about getting Alison's car to run long enough to get them back into town.

The hood was yawning open over him, like a tamed circus lion. He was staring into it with an unenlightened expression on his face, like a man who had met his match and wasn't happy about it.

She moved closer to him. "Anything?"

Jimmy shook his head. There was no point in hoping that he'd suddenly be hit with a burst of automotive know-how. It wasn't going to happen. His expertise ended with sticking the key into the ignition and turning it.

"The battery's dead," he confirmed. "I can heal a patient, but I haven't a clue how to bring a dead battery around." He closed the hood again, not that it mattered. "We'd need Kevin for this."

He turned from the car to look at her. Why wasn't he the least bit worried? he wondered. Where was all this inner calm coming from? "How about you? Are you one of those resourceful girls who can fix the engine of a 747 with a bobby pin and a well-placed kick?"

Stepping back into the shelter of the doorway, out of the wind's reach, she shook her head. "The only kick I can think of placing has nothing to do with a 747 or a dead car."

Abandoning the defunct vehicle, he turned his attention to April. "This sounds like it might be interesting."

The fact that he seemed completely unfazed by their predicament meant that the man either had nerves of steel, or brains of mush and didn't comprehend the possibilities they could be facing. "I meant I could kick myself for not staying at the village."

He wasn't about to let her upbraid herself, not when it was such a supreme waste of energy. "You had no way of knowing this was going to hit so fast."

April shook her head, not placated. "But I should have."

He glanced up at the sky. The dark clouds were there, but in the distance. "It looks like it's letting up a little. Maybe we should try to get back."

April knew the danger in thinking that way. Storms hit without warning. If they were out in the open, they could easily die of exposure. She pointed to the darker clouds. However slowly, they were on the move. "It's just a reprieve. There's another storm coming soon. I don't want us to be out in the open when it hits."

He accepted the verdict. "All right, then let's go back inside and wait this out. I don't know about you but I'm getting cold and I need to warm up." He looked at her significantly.

At this point, she could read him like a book. "You know, at this rate you're going to wear yourself out before they find us."

Hooking his thumb into the belt loop of her jeans, he gently pulled her across the threshold and inside the cabin. "Never happen."

Exhausted, her body damp with the sweat of lovemaking, April fell back against the floor, too spent to even take a deep breath. The cabin felt as if it was spinning out of control.

Just like her, out of control.

Once we get back, it'll all go back to the way it was, she promised, trying to placate the skittish nerves that kept surfacing.

A sound penetrated her consciousness. It was a distant, rumbling noise.

An engine?

Her eyes flew open and she turned toward Jimmy. His expression gave no indication that he'd heard anything. When he started to say something to her, she quickly put her hand to his mouth to silence him.

"Listen, do you hear anything?" She looked up toward the ceiling as if doing that could somehow help tell her what she was hearing.

He kissed her fingertips. "Just the beating of my heart."

She pulled her hand away. There, she'd heard it again. "No, I'm serious."

Jimmy listened. There was nothing. "What do you hear?"

"An engine. A motor." Or maybe it was something else. "Something. It's in the distance, but it's getting louder."

He still didn't hear it, but didn't question that she did. "You've got better hearing than a bat, then. But that's where the comparison ends."

He was just humoring her, she thought. Undoubtedly he probably assumed she was so desperate to be found that she was imagining car engines. But she was hearing something. And it was getting louder.

Max. Max was coming for them. Oh, my God, she had to get dressed quickly. April reached for her clothes. "No, I—"

The next thing she knew, the door was being pushed open. Sucking in her breath, April had only enough time to grab the moth-eaten blanket and pull it to her. And then she was looking up at her brother's face, trying to ignore the fact that Shayne and Ike were right behind him.

Max looked by turns surprised, relieved, and then greatly amused.

The initial protective instinct faded a second after rising. No one could make April do what she didn't want to do. That meant she wanted to be with this man. After resigning himself to the idea that April was never going to find anyone she would trust enough to become vulnerable with, seeing her in this sort of a situation made Max want to smile.

It took an effort to keep the expression from his lips. April would have his head.

"And here I was, worried that you might be freezing to death." He shook his head, relief washing over him in long, comforting waves. She was safe, that was all that mattered right now. "I should have known you'd find a way to start your own fire."

Temporarily at a loss, April raised her chin, fervently wishing she could make herself invisible by merely closing her eyes, the way she'd once believed as a child.

With as much dignity as she could muster, she said, "Would you give us a moment, please?"

"Take all the time you want, darlin'," Ike drawled, turning his back to the pair. He caught Shayne's eye and winked. "We're just very glad to find that you're both alive. Really alive," he emphasized. "You've got no idea what Shayne's been putting himself through, thinking that something might have happened to you because you went to the village instead of him.''

His jeans on, Jimmy padded across the floor to retrieve the boots he'd abandoned near the door.

"Why wouldn't we be alive?" Sitting on the floor, he began pulling on his boots. "In case you hadn't noticed—" he looked at Max "—your sister's one hell of a woman. She doesn't go all to pieces at the first sign of an emergency the way a lot of other people—male and female," he added for her benefit, "would in her situation. She's a survivor. That gives anyone with her more than a fighting chance.''

Finished hurrying into her clothes, April looked at Jimmy in mute surprise. Other than Max when she'd managed to pin him down, no man had ever willingly given her her due. That Jimmy did stirred a warm pride within her she didn't know what to do with.

"Well, in that case," Ike suggested, tongue in cheek, "maybe we should just leave." He waved a hand at himself and the other two men.

"No, you're here, you might as well be of some use." The smile that came to April's lips was apologetic. "I guess what I mean is that we really did need rescuing. The car won't start. There was no place to house it and I think the battery's frozen." She looked at Luc. It was his car, after all. "I'm sorry."

Luc had lived in Hades all of his life. It wasn't anything that he hadn't encountered before. "No problem. I'll have your sister look at it. If anyone can make it run, June can.''

Max suddenly remembered the others. "June's out

looking for you, too. Hell, we've got half the village out looking for the two of you. I'd better get on the radio and see if I can get in touch with any of them, tell them the search's over." He hurried out the door.

April pressed her lips together, contrite. She'd forgotten about that, forgotten how everyone in Hades always pulled together, no matter what their differences, whenever anyone was in trouble. It was as if they were all members of one large, rambling family. No matter what, they looked out for one another.

She supposed that was the one thing she'd missed, being away from here. Shoving her hands into her pockets, she looked at Ike and Shayne. Apologies didn't come easily to her, but she'd never shirked what she felt was her responsibility.

"Thanks for coming out. I'm sorry to have put everyone through this."

Jimmy slipped his hand onto her shoulder in a manner she found both possessive and oddly comforting, though she tried to block out the latter.

"It was my fault," he told them. "April wanted to start back, but I made her wait while I stopped to have a cup of coffee at Jack's house. We would have beaten the storm back if it hadn't been for me."

She looked at him, puzzled. Why was he lying for her? She didn't need anyone running interference for her, even though she should have known better and hurried him along. "No, I—"

Shayne didn't want to hear any more apologies. It was behind them now. "Well, you're all right now so there's no harm done." He opened the door to leave. "Next time, bring a thermos."

"There's not going to be a next time," April told them. Checking the fireplace to make sure the fire was out, she nodded at Jimmy. "His vacation is almost over and he'll be going back."

"Forgot about that." Ike looked at his cousin's brother-in-law. "I guess I just started getting used to you and thought you were one of us." His eyes swept toward April. "You, too."

She met the comment with ambivalent feelings. Part of her wanted to reaffirm that there was no doubt that she was no longer one of them. That she'd outgrown this hayseed of a town. But another part wanted to take umbrage at being dismissed so cavalierly, because, God help her, she *was* part of them. And a piece of her always would be.

She was beginning to wonder if that was a blessing or not.

She didn't want to think about it. "Let's get back," she urged. "Gran must be frantic." And then it occurred to her. Hurrying to where Max stood by the plane, completing his radio message, she grabbed his arm to get his attention. "If June's out looking for me, who's staying with Gran?"

Max replaced the receiver. "Mrs. Kellogg," he told her.

Her eyes widened. The name conjured up vivid pictures of a dour old woman in her mind. "The old grocer's wife? The one who started the last fire?" In one of her long, newsy letters, her grandmother had written to her how part of the emporium Luc now owned had burned down. The fire had threatened the Salty, as well, before it had been put out by the volunteer fire department. It had begun because Mrs. Kellogg had forgotten about a pot of soup she'd left cooking on the range. "My God, what was June thinking?"

"That she didn't want to lose her sister, would be my guess," Jimmy said, slipping his arm around her shoulders. He noticed that she stiffened at his touch. Their idyllic time, he decided, was over. A sadness blended with another feeling that surprised him. It was the feeling that came over him when he faced a challenge.

She didn't need him running interference or making excuses for her family. "Let's go," April ordered, climbing into the plane.

"What about the box of canned goods?" Jimmy wanted to know. They'd eaten very little during their stay here, rationing the cans in case they would have to last a long time. Most of their time together had been occupied by matters other than food.

"Leave them for the next person who's marooned out here," she said, strapping herself in. She looked expectantly at Shayne who was still standing outside the plane with the others. "What are we waiting for? Let's go!"

Amusement creased Ike's lips. "You heard the lady."

"You know," Max said as he climbed in behind Jimmy, "I'd forgotten how much the sound of your voice could make the hairs on the back of my neck stand up."

"We'll reminisce about that later." Leaning forward, she gripped the back of the pilot's seat, as if that could somehow make the plane take off. "I want to get back to Gran before something happens to her."

"She's heartier than you think," was all Max said as Shayne started the engine.

Since she was the first one on the plane, per force, April was the last one out when they landed. As soon as her feet hit the patchy snow-covered ground, she was off and running for the post office.

"You know, if you break your leg, you're not going to do anyone any good," Max called after her, shaking his head.

She didn't bother acknowledging him. She was too intent on trying to fight off the bad feeling she had, the feeling that something had happened to her grandmother while she had been up there in the cabin, getting lost in Jimmy's arms. What she should have done, she upbraided herself, was try to figure out a way they could have gotten back. Or at least gotten word to someone. That both options had been impossible to follow through on only made her frustration that much greater.

Bursting into the post office, her lungs screaming from her effort, she looked frantically around, fearing the worst.

Her grandmother was behind the counter, just the way she'd been for nearly half a century, looking very intent on sorting mail. She looked up the moment she heard the door open, hope creasing her brow.

"April!" Her hand pressing heavily down on the counter for support, she struggled to her feet. "I knew you were all right. I just knew it.'' Beaming, blinking back tears, Ursula opened her arms wide.

April flew into them and suddenly found herself propelled back to her childhood, where Gran's arms had always formed a welcoming haven, no matter what was going on in the world outside her arms.

Blinking back her own unfounded tears, April searched the older woman's face. ''Are you all right?''

''I am now, now that you're here.'' She wiped away a tear with the back of her wrist then looked over April's head at the men entering the post office. ''Are you all right, Doc?''

''Never better.'' Coming forward, Jimmy stopped by April. ''Had your granddaughter watching out for me.''

Ursula nodded knowingly as she looked at April. ''Then you were in good hands.''

''I'll say,'' Max muttered under his breath, only to be given a dirty look by April.

Immediately interested, Ursula cocked her head. ''How's that?''

''Nothing,'' April said quickly. ''Max is just being Max.'' She looked at her grandmother. ''You should be in bed.''

Ursula glanced over toward the back stairs. ''I was too restless to stay in bed. But I think I could do with a bit of rest now that you're back.''

That Gran gave in so easily worried her. ''Want help up the stairs?'' She took her grandmother's arm.

Very gently, Ursula pulled herself free. ''No, I'll be fine.'' And then she hesitated. ''Maybe the doc would like to help me up the stairs.''

April didn't like the sound of that.

Chapter Fifteen

"April?"

Her grandmother's voice penetrated the restless haze that had been pressing down on her all night, just as it had the past three nights, ever since she and Jimmy had been rescued and returned to Hades. With little sleep to her credit, her temper was short, even with Gran. Right now, April figured she wasn't even good company for a wolverine.

No matter what excuse she'd silently rendered, she'd felt herself becoming vulnerable back when they'd been snowed in. Vulnerable to the point that her emotions had come all unraveled for the first time in years. And, for the first time in her life, she'd forgotten to keep them under control. She'd allowed herself to react to Jimmy, to let some part of her think "What if...?"

Except that she knew all about what-ifs. If she fell in love, really in love, what would happen would be that she'd end up just like her mother and countless other women who'd loved and lost and suddenly no longer remembered how to place one foot in front of the other to get through a day. April knew herself well enough to know that she wasn't one who did things by half measures. If she loved, she'd love completely and if she lost, as she knew she would, then the very heart would be cut out of her.

It very nearly was when her father had abandoned them. How much worse would it be if it was the man who she'd given herself to, body and soul?

She wasn't about to allow herself to find out. This policy of evasion she'd adopted would see her through until Jimmy left Hades. She only had two more days to play hide-and-seek with him and then he'd be gone, on his way to Seattle. And she would go on just as she had before, just a little wiser.

And she was going to make damn sure this kind of thing wasn't going to happen again. No other man would ever be allowed to creep into her mind and remain there, haunting every thought she had.

In the meantime, she needed support and cooperation. That meant not having to put up with her grandmother's continuous testimonials about "the new doc." New doc. As if he was staying here. It was obvious that her grandmother had taken leave of her senses and become smitten with a man one third her age. A man who, for some reason, Gran somehow saw her with. As if that would ever happen. April was far too bright for that. Sure she'd gotten a little giddy, a little carried away, but she was over that.

If she hadn't been, she would have found some way to see him in the last three days. And she hadn't. She'd avoided him as if he were all seven of the Bible plagues all rolled into one.

Raising herself up on her elbows, she called out to her grandmother, "Gran, please, I'm tired and I don't want to hear any more arguments about how wonderful 'the doc' is. If he's so great, you marry him. I hear Seattle's great this time of year."

"April." The voice was thin, reedy and breathless before it cracked.

April bolted upright, listening, alert. She didn't like the sound of that. Something was very wrong.

Forgoing her robe, she hurried into her grandmother's room down the tiny hall. Ursula was still in bed, too weak to sit up on her own. April turned on the light and bit back the cry of dismay that materialized on her lips. Her grandmother's face was ashen and she was clutching her chest.

With panic slashing at her on all fronts, April dropped to her knees. She tried very hard to keep her voice calm to prevent her grandmother from becoming agitated. "Where does it hurt, Gran?"

Watery eyes turned to her. April saw the fear mirrored there that she was trying to bank down. Her grandmother wasn't one given to complaining. "I can't catch my breath, April."

"I'll get Shayne."

Reaching for the telephone, she started dialing before she realized that there was no sound on the other end. The phones were dead again for the third time in four days. Another storm had hit them this afternoon, just as furious as its sister had been several days before.

April unsuccessfully swallowed an oath.

"It's all right," Ursula murmured. "This'll pass, and I'll be fine."

April wasn't so sure and she certainly wasn't about to bet her grandmother's life on it. Her first thought was to go and bring Shayne back with her, but she didn't want to leave Gran alone. If the unthinkable happened, she didn't want her dying without someone beside her.

"Sure you will," she said with far more conviction than she felt. "But just to be on the safe side, I'm going to take you to him."

Ursula's breathing had steadied a little, but she didn't feel strong enough to make it on her own power. She held on to April's hand tightly. "I really don't know if I can—"

"Yes, you can," April said firmly. "Look at me, Gran." April looked into the eyes of the woman who had been her entire world after she and her siblings had been orphaned. Never mind that she had been determined to help raise the others and declared herself a responsible, independent person, it had been Gran who'd always been her rock. "Now you are going to walk out of here and we're going to see Shayne. I'm going to help you so you don't have to be afraid."

"I'm not afraid," Ursula lied. She rubbed small, concentric circles on her chest. "I'm just being foolish. It's probably nothing more than just indigestion."

Very slowly, April helped her grandmother into a sitting position, using her shoulder as leverage to give Ursula some support. "Fine, then I'll get you a box of antacid tablets—after I hear Shayne tell me it's indigestion."

Dangling her feet over the side of the bed, Ursula watched as April quickly put socks and shoes on her feet. "But, April, we'll wake him up. It's the middle of the night."

April quickly threw an outfit together for her grandmother to keep her warm. "This is Alaska, Gran. It's the middle of the night six months out of the year," she quipped. "No one'll notice."

"Shayne, open up. It's April!"

It had taken her exactly three minutes to throw on her own clothes and then ten to get her grandmother down the stairs and into the car. By the time she'd closed the vehicle door and turned on the ignition, she was almost as drenched with perspiration as the time she'd gone photographing alligators in the Bayou in August.

When her grandmother's breathing became labored, April had driven like someone possessed to Shayne's house.

The front door to Shayne's restored two-story house finally flew open. Blinking his eyes, trying to focus and clear his brain of sleep, Shayne looked at April a second before recognition set in. Behind him, his wife Sydney was just coming down the stairs.

Shayne could barely make out the vehicle in the background. "April, what's wrong?"

"It's Gran." April fought back the wave of hysteria that came at her with a vengeance. "I think she's having a heart attack."

Shayne was already crossing to the car in his slippers, unmindful of the newly fallen snow. "Let's bring her inside."

A preliminary examination of the older woman with April hovering anxiously in the room proved inconclusive. It looked to Shayne as if April was right about the minor heart attack, but he didn't want to speculate without more data.

Leaving Ursula with Sydney to help her get dressed, he took April aside. "I'm going to have to take your grandmother to the clinic, April, before I can tell you with any certainty just what's going on." He glanced over his shoulder toward his patient. "But I think you're right, I think she did have a minor episode." A gentle smile moved his lips. "That's a euphemism for a heart attack that doesn't leave you flat on your back."

Turning around, he crossed back to Ursula. "Looks like I finally get to do that echocardiogram you've been putting off, Ursula." Shayne looked at his wife. "Syd, wake Mac up," he told her, referring to their oldest son. "Tell him he gets to be in charge until we get back—and not to let power go to his head." He saw her look at him quizzically. "I'm going to need your help with Ursula."

"I'm coming with you," April cut in, eager to be of any use. "Sydney doesn't have to—"

She got no further. "I need you to go get Alison,"

Shayne told her. "And more importantly, her brother."

The first thing April thought of was that Jimmy was a surgeon. She could feel her heart beginning to pound as anxiety returned. She turned so that her grandmother couldn't see her lips. "Are you going to have to operate?" she asked, lowering her voice.

Shayne shook his head. "I don't know yet. I really hope not." He needed to get dressed. "Tell them to meet us at the clinic."

April paused only long enough to take her grandmother's hands in her own and squeeze them. Gran gave her a brave smile as she wrapped her long, thin fingers around hers. A sliver of panic shot through April. Her grandmother's grip had never felt this weak before.

She bent her head, her lips by her grandmother's ear. "Hang on, Gran, we're going to get you through this. I swear we will," she said fiercely. "I'm not going to let anything happen to you."

April hurried out, praying she hadn't just lied to her grandmother.

She wasn't sure just how she made it. One moment she was in front of Shayne's house, the next, she was bringing the car to a screeching halt in front of the single-story rambling house Luc had had built for Alison after they were married.

April was so filled with tears, she was afraid she was going to explode.

That's not going to help Gran, she warned herself, getting out. She nearly slipped on the ground. The storm had swelled again, bringing with it more snow. The wind whipped across her face as she banged on the front door, forgoing niceties.

It was Jimmy, his guest room located just off the living room, who got to the door first. Wearing blue jeans he'd hastily dragged on and nothing else, he was combing the hair out of his eyes with one hand as he opened the front door with the other.

The moment he saw her, he knew it had to do with her grandmother. April's eyes were almost wild with fear and bright with tears she was holding prisoner. Instinct had him grabbing her arms, afraid she would fall at the slightest provocation.

"April, is it your grandmother?"

He knew, she thought, swallowing, a lump in her throat temporarily rendering her unable to speak. She nodded her head vigorously.

Jimmy moved her aside, looking toward her car. "She's here?"

April caught his arm before he could walk out. "No, Shayne's taking her to the clinic. He—I think she's had a heart attack. He wanted me to come get you and Alison." She heard noise in the background and voices, but couldn't focus on them. The panic was threatening to overwhelm her. Still holding his arm, she wasn't aware of squeezing hard. "Jimmy, she can't—"

"She won't," he told her firmly, cutting in. There was no point in looking at odds or reality, or saying that that they were in some out-of-the-way place devoid of the latest technology rather than in the middle of a large hospital where her chances, if Ursula was actually having a heart attack, would be far better. April didn't need to hear that. She needed something to hold on to, if only for a little while. Anything else would have been self-serving and cruel. He kissed her forehead gently. "Just wait a second, I'll get Alison—"

The kindness nearly undid her. She fared far better in turmoil, with people shouting around her. April swallowed a sob.

"Already here." Alison came up behind him. She'd heard enough to let her know what was going on. "I heard," she assured Jimmy, her hand on his shoulder. She offered April an encouraging smile. "All I need is a minute to get my clothes." She was hurrying away before she finished her statement.

April looked as if she was going to shatter any second, he thought, looking at her. The reserved woman who had all but frozen him out these past three days with little to no explanation had vanished. The woman he'd fallen for in the cabin stood in her place.

His heart went out to April but he knew that pity was the last thing she'd welcome.

So he gave her an order, instinctively knowing that would work far better. Pointing to her car, he instructed, "Go start the engine."

She did what he told without a word.

April looked at her watch.

It had been two hours since she'd watched the doors to the small operating room in the rear close. What were they doing in there? Too much time had elapsed.

It shouldn't be taking this long, should it?

Alone in the outer office since Sydney had returned to her children, April didn't know what to do with herself. With the phone lines still down, Sydney had offered to go get both Max and June, but April had convinced her not to. There was no point in all three of them going through this agony. It was bad enough she had to endure it.

Gran, she'd told Sydney as the other woman left, was going to be fine.

Sydney had nodded. "She couldn't be in better hands."

Shayne had used the brand-new echocardiogram machine that had been a philanthropic gift from Luc's friend, a former resident of Hades, to discern that Gran had a dangerous blockage of one of the main arteries leading to her heart. Normally with a blockage of that nature, they'd lose no time in performing a by-pass. But Shayne didn't have the necessary equipment to successfully perform the surgery.

April had paled at the news. "So what are you going to do?"

It was Jimmy who had suggested doing an angioplasty as a stop-gap procedure. "That way, her heart can sustain the necessary blood flow until there's a break in the weather and she can be flown to Anchorage." He'd looked toward her as next of kin.

"Do it," she'd said without hesitation.

They were in there now, Jimmy, Shayne and Alison, with her grandmother's life literally in their hands while she sat out here, climbing out of her skin, counting minutes on a clock with hands that seemingly refused to move.

She was pretty useless, April thought angrily, up-braiding herself as she paced the length of the waiting room. She'd been in Hades for more than two weeks and in that time she'd been unable to convince her grandmother to go to Providence Hospital for a more thorough exam.

Damn it. April wiped a tear away from cheek. She hadn't even been able to force her grandmother to have the echocardiogram done after Shayne had gotten the machine in. If she had bullied her into taking the test, then this wouldn't be happening. They would have gotten Gran to the hospital in time to do the surgery properly.

Why hadn't she been able to convince Gran?

Because she'd been too busy showing Jimmy around, April thought, disgusted with herself. If she hadn't been so self-absorbed, so wrapped up in having a good time, then—

The door to the rear room opened. Like a shot, April was there, eagerly pouncing on Shayne. Afraid of what he might tell her. Praying it was good news.

"Well? Is she—?"

Pulling down his surgical mask, Shayne smiled at her. "She's out of danger for the moment. There are times when an angioplasty is enough, but in your grandmother's case, she'll still need to go to Anchorage to have that by-pass done."

That was understood. Tentative relief began poking around within her. "How soon will she have to go?"

"No immediate rush now, thanks to Jimmy."

Weary, Shayne glanced over his shoulder to the back room. There was no doubt in his mind that it'd been a blessing, having Jimmy here. The last time he'd seen an angioplasty done, he'd been part of a medical firm on Park Avenue. Working alongside the younger man had taken Shayne back to when he and his brother had run the clinic here together.

"Once Ursula recovers from her anesthesia, we can make further arrangements." His smile broadened, guessing at what April must have gone through. "Don't worry, your grandmother has a great constitution. And it didn't hurt having a great surgeon in there, either. We were lucky to have Jimmy."

Hearing him as he came out of the room, Jimmy shrugged. "You would have done the procedure if I wasn't here."

"Point was, you were, and you are far more up on the procedure than I am." Shayne had always given people their due. "Fact is, you're up on a lot more procedures than I am here. I could really use a man like you."

"So you keep telling me." Exhausted after operating on what had amounted to a near sleepless night, Jimmy still found the strength to laugh. In the past week and a half, Shayne had never missed an opportunity to tell him how satisfying it was to practice medicine in a place where he was really needed, where patients were more than just names on a roster. "I don't think I've ever felt quite as wanted as I do right now."

Stripping off his surgical scrubs, Shayne set them on a chair. "Well, I certainly can't bribe you with money, but there's no beating the satisfaction. Think about it,'' were his parting words before he returned to his patient.

There were no words she could say to this man she'd snubbed and ignored for the last few days that would begin to express her gratitude to him for saving her grandmother's life. Any attempt just seemed to get stuck in her throat.

Clearing it, she indicated the back room. ''May I see her?''

''Sure.'' Shedding his mask and tossing it on the chair on top of Shayne's scrubs, he started to lead her back. ''Follow me.''

April caught his arm. When he looked at her quizzically, she blurted the first thing that came to mind. Better something than nothing. ''I don't know how to thank you.''

He smiled at her. ''Don't worry about it. Your eyes already did.''

Linking his fingers through hers, Jimmy led her into the room where Shayne normally performed the minor surgeries that were a day-to-day occurrence in Hades. Clean, pristine, the room didn't look as if anything more sophisticated than simple suturing could be undertaken here.

But it had. And she was eternally grateful.

April caught her breath as she looked down at her grandmother, her eyes closed, looking ghostly pale against the white sheets around her.

Gran was so still. Without realizing it, April squeezed Jimmy's hand.

Alison adjusted the white blanket covering the woman. ''She'll sleep probably until morning. I'll stay with her,'' Alison told April, then looked at her brother. ''Why don't you take April home?''

April didn't want to leave. She wanted to stay here. In case Gran needed her. ''I—''

Jimmy was taking her arm as Shayne cut short her protest. ''Doctor's order.''

April looked from one face to another. She couldn't argue with all three of them and she didn't want to seem ungrateful. ''Maybe I am a little tired.''

''Now you're being sensible,'' Jimmy told her. He picked up the jacket she didn't remember shedding and slipped it onto her shoulders.

April let herself be led out, feeling oddly numb all over.

''We'll use your car,'' Jimmy was saying. She realized he was holding his hand out for her keys. It took her a minute to locate them.

It was as if every bone in her body suddenly sagged as she sat in the passenger seat. She was exhausted, yet wired. Stealing a glance toward Jimmy's profile as he started the car, she let out a long, slow breath.

There was a lot of unfinished business between them. To have left it up in the air was cowardly.

Like her father when he'd just left them one morning.

It wasn't fair to Jimmy. She needed to explain things, to make them right. Especially now since he'd saved her grandmother.

But yet when she looked for the words, nothing came. Her mind felt blank. Numb and blank.

What did she say? How did she start? How did she end?

The car had stopped moving. They were at her door, she realized, bewildered at how the trip could have gone so fast.

"We're here," he told her.

She nodded, getting out. Walking to the door on someone else's legs. Nothing felt as if it belonged to her. Not her body, not her feelings. Not her thoughts. Everything was jumbled, disoriented.

Sensing her tension, Jimmy stopped at her door and looked at her. She shouldn't be alone. "Want me to stay with you for a while?"

"No."

The single word came out like a defensive line-backer barreling over him. Jimmy backed away. "All right. Good night, then."

"Yes."

He turned around to look at her, waiting for a final ruling. Dragging her hand through her hair, April offered him a rueful smile.

"I'm sorry, it's just that—when I thought about Gran dying and that it was my fault—"

He came back to her side. "How could it have been your fault?"

April unlocked the front door. Didn't he see? "I didn't make her go to Anchorage. That was the reason I came back here and I just let her float along, accepting her excuses, thinking that maybe I had made too big a deal of it after all. I should have known better—"

He saw the anguish in her eyes. "April, you can't bully everybody."

Her hand on the doorknob, she laughed shortly.

"That's just it, I do, I bully everyone, but when it counted—" When it counted, she thought, she'd failed. Miserably. She knew her grandmother had needed to get further medical attention and she'd let her down.

Sympathy stirred within him. Jimmy caressed her face. "April, you're not in charge of the world, or even of your grandmother. People make mistakes and you can't second guess every situation."

She wasn't going to allow him to whitewash this for her. "But I came here to take care of her and I did a lousy job—"

Jimmy placed his finger to her lips, stopping her. "You got her to the clinic in time," he reminded her. "And in the long run, that's all that counts. You saved her life as much as I did, April. More, because if you hadn't brought her in time, I couldn't have operated on her."

"You do have a hell of a bedside manner," she said softly.

His eyes crinkled as he smiled at her. "See, I told you I did."

She pressed her lips together as she finally turned the doorknob and opened the front door. It was dark within the post office.

As dark as she'd felt inside, sitting in the clinic, waiting to hear if Gran was alive or dead.

Jimmy heard her shallow breathing though he sensed she was trying very hard to not let go. He knew she wouldn't appreciate his seeing her cry, but knew, too, that right now, she needed not to be the strong one. For one moment in time, April needed to release the hold she had on her emotions.

He touched her shoulder. "April."

Very gently, he turned her around to face him. Angrily defensive, she jerked her face away, but with his thumb beneath her chin, he forced her to turn around and look at him. "It's okay to cry."

"I never cry," she told him.

The next moment, she did.

Jimmy held her close to him as she sobbed. Her body trembled as huge, body-racking sobs shook it. Jimmy stroked her back, then, picking her up into his arms, he walked slowly to the rear of the room. Carrying her up the stairs, he murmured soft endearments that somehow managed to penetrate through the haze of tears, guilt and relief that wound themselves tightly around her.

Chapter Sixteen

The instant Jimmy brought her to her room and set her down on her bed, it was as if a dam had broken loose within her. April forgot about everything else, about the promises she'd made to herself. About protecting herself.

She couldn't be alone tonight. And the only person she wanted to be with was Jimmy.

April caught his arm as he began to straighten, bringing him closer to her.

"Stay with me," she said quietly.

Thinking she only wanted him to hold her, Jimmy sat on the edge of the bed and gathered her against him. "I'm not going anywhere." Leaning over, he lightly brushed his lips on her forehead.

April reached for him. He saw the silent plea in her

eyes, the need for comfort. The need for someone to help her make the world disappear.

The need for him.

Even if he'd thought of resisting, he couldn't. Not when he'd spent the past few days trying to talk himself into not wanting her and knowing that he was lying. It had seemed ironic to him, Murphy's Law at its finest and most diabolical. The one woman he'd actually wanted in his life, the one woman he was willing to rethink his entire philosophy of living for, and she'd suddenly done an about-face and made it clear that she hadn't wanted him.

But now she did and there was no room for pride, for principles, or for watching his back.

He brought his mouth down to hers and kissed her with all the longing that had haunted him the past three days. The past eternity.

It was different this time, different than the time they had spent in the cabin. Separated by several days, it seemed as if that had all happened in another lifetime. That was child's play. This was deadly serious.

There was a wild urgency that seized them both, far more intense than had existed even their first time together. His pulse raced as she kissed him over and over again. If there was an aggressor in this, it was April.

It felt as if she was possessed and desperately in need of purging herself of all thought, of everything but this exhilarating feeling coursing through her veins like a continuous plunge down a roller-coaster incline that ran on to infinity.

She made love to him in an abandoned frenzy, as

if the end of the world was at their doorstep, waiting to dissolve them both.

He felt the change in her immediately. It was all he could do to keep up with her. She'd taken his breath away the very first moment. Far from lightning in a bottle, he felt as if he was holding lightning in his hand.

"It's okay, baby, it's okay," he murmured against her ear as he felt her lips against his throat. Shafts of desire, sharp and strong, shot through him. "We can take this slow."

But they couldn't.

It was as if he had boarded a runaway toboggan and could only hold on for the ride of his life. The desperation that was driving April had taken control of them both.

The pleasure escalated to an agonizing sweetness that was both her jailer and her prisoner. Delicious sensations battered her body as she felt his lips trail over her limbs, heightening the fire that had been ignited from the first moment.

Unable to wait any longer, she snaked her body over his, reversing their positions. Hands joined with his, nails digging into his flesh, she fit herself over him and initiated the last phase of their lovemaking.

The choice of timing taken from him, he began to move in a tempo that outstripped hers until they reached the highest peak together, their sweat-drenched bodies collapsing against one another like the sides of a bellows once the energy was spent.

The euphoria of afterglow clinging to him, Jimmy lightly caressed her body as it rested on top of his. If anyone had asked, he would have said he was content to remain that way until the last stroke of forever.

Her heart quickened as she felt his fingertips glide along her back.

"I love you."

Startled by what she'd just allowed to slip out, April sat bolt upright, afraid that he'd heard her.

One look at his face told her he had.

Maybe he'd only imagined it. Maybe he'd wanted to hear the words so badly, had harbored them himself for a while now, he'd actually thought he'd heard her say them.

Gripping her shoulders, he looked at her. "What did you say?"

"Nothing." Upset with herself, with her own weakness, April shrugged off his hands and moved away from him. "Nothing at all."

He sat up, his eyes pinning her. "Yes, you did. You said you loved me."

"You're hearing things," she denied heatedly. Angry at the senseless slip she'd allowed, April looked frantically around for the clothes she hadn't been able to wait to shed from her body. "Look, this was a mistake." All of it. She shouldn't have let him stay.

Let? she silently mocked herself. More like beg him to stay. Damn it, what was wrong with her? Was she really just as pathetic as her mother? Didn't she have any pride? Any sense?

Quickly, he pulled on his jeans, sensing that in her present frame of mind, April could take off at any moment. "I don't think that was a mistake."

Jerking on the oversize sweater she'd thrown on

when she'd rushed her grandmother to Shayne's house, April swung around to look at him. "I should know what I said or didn't say."

Her eyes looked like blue flames. The rest of her, with the bottom of the sweater skimming the tops of her thighs, looked delectable. It was a struggle to keep his mind focused on the argument at hand.

And he had to keep focused if he didn't want to lose her again. Permanently this time. "Maybe it's time you stopped running."

The single word touched off an explosion within her. She was so angry at him, she could have spit. "What do you mean, 'running'?"

He reached for his shirt without really looking at it, afraid that if he looked away, she would run off. Maybe that wasn't realistic, but neither was the magnitude of what he was feeling. His parents' love, his father had liked telling him when he was small, had come slowly. This had come like a fireball out of the sky.

"You are not your mother, April. And I am not your father."

For a second, she was too stunned to move or to speak. Her eyes narrowed as she fisted her hands at her sides. "Just what are you suggesting?"

At the risk of having her take a swing at him, he crossed to her and put his hands on her shoulders. She stiffened and tried to jerk away, but he tightened his grip. "That if I can get over this feeling that everything's finite and make a grab at what's in front of me, so can you."

Easy for him to say. He could walk away. Would

walk away. While she was left with pieces that would never reassemble themselves.

With one unexpected move, she yanked herself away from him. "We *did* grab at it," she told him, her voice rising. "We had an affair and now it's over."

"Well, maybe I'm not done with it," he shouted at her back. "Maybe I want it to go on."

Her heart pounding, she turned from the doorway, aborting her escape. "For how long? You're leaving, remember?"

He'd been giving it a lot of thought these past few days, ever since he'd returned from the village. Shayne was right, there was something seductively gratifying in being the possible difference between life and death for a patient who had no other recourse. The surgery he'd performed on Ursula had only pushed the balance a little further.

"That's just it," he said, his voice lowering to normal again, "maybe I'm not."

She stared at him. He was staying? No, it was just a ruse, a whim. And besides, it didn't make a difference to her plans.

"Well, I am." April tossed her head, trying to add weight to convictions that were turning strangely light and translucent. "Just as soon as I'm sure Gran's well and taken care of."

He wanted to hold her. To make her stay put and to admit to what she was feeling. To what he *knew* she was feeling. Instead he remained where he was. She had to take that final giant step herself.

"You don't have to leave."

"Yes," she retorted fiercely, something almost frantic underlining her tone, "I do."

Maybe this *was* useless, he thought. He couldn't force her to do anything. It wouldn't count. "I forgot, you have to run."

It was like waving a red flag in front of a charging bull. "I am *not* running."

He knew otherwise. She'd been running all of her adult life. Running from something that could make her happy. He didn't care about her past, but he did care about her future, even if he wasn't included. Suddenly he understood exactly what his father had felt about his mother and it was worth everything to feel this way.

"Then stay put someplace for longer than it takes to snap a roll of film." He came closer to her, tentatively reaching out his hand and brushing back a strand of hair from her cheek. "Stay put where you're needed and wanted. And loved."

She wanted to. Heaven help her, she wanted to. But she was afraid. Afraid to stay. Afraid to love. His eyes were holding her still.

"Why are you staying?"

"Because I'm needed here more than I am back home," he told her honestly. "For the first time in my life, I feel like I really make a difference." He smiled, thinking of the man who had tried so diligently to talk him into remaining. "Because maybe Shayne needs a break once in a while so he can kiss his wife and hug his kids and feel like a man instead of a doctor." He was caressing her cheek now, smiling warmly into her eyes. "And because this is your home."

She tried to shrug him off and found herself immobilized, not because he was holding her tightly but because she couldn't make herself initiate the break.

"What's that got to do with anything?"

"Because if you leave, you'll be back." He was as sure of that as he was of his own abilities as a surgeon. "And maybe during one of those return trips, I'll be able to convince you to stay."

April laughed shortly, feeling tears of frustration and hopelessness gathering in her eyes. She was losing ground and she was afraid. "So we can have a long affair instead of a fling?"

"No," he told her softly, his fingers playing along the planes of her face, "so we can have a marriage and children. I want kids, April." He felt his heart swelling. There was a chance. She was weakening. "I want kids with your face stamped on them, with your stubbornness and grace and my determination."

"I've got determination," she sniffed as she felt herself losing ground at a prodigious rate.

"I've got more." He leaned his forehead against hers. "Because I'm willing to wait this out until you say yes."

She could all but feel the white flag in her hand. "And if I never do?"

"Then it'll be a hell of a game." When he smiled like that, she could feel the warmth clear into her chest. "But you will."

For the sake of her pride, she tried to keep the game up a little longer. "You're sure."

"I'm sure."

Damn, but she loved him, she thought as the hopelessness mysteriously began to slip away to be replaced by something stronger. Something with depth and breadth and substance. "And you've never been wrong."

He pretended to think a moment. "Once. In 1995. October twenty-seventh."

Unable to hold it back, she started to laugh. "You're crazy, you know that?"

It was going to be all right, he thought, relieved. Jimmy slipped his arms around her. "I am," he agreed, nuzzling her neck. "About you."

He was making it very hard for her to think. "So, if I said yes—"

Jimmy raised his head and looked into her eyes. "When," he corrected.

"If," she insisted. After all, a woman had to have some kind of pride. "You'd be willing to give up everything and stay here?"

"I already am staying here," he pointed out. "And the way I see it, I'm not giving up everything." Jimmy looked at her significantly. "I'm gaining it."

The stubborn streak that had seen her through so much in her life egged her on a little further before the inevitable surrender. "You drive a hard bargain, you know that?"

He smiled, slipping his hands beneath the edges of her sweater, his fingers grazing the cool flesh of her thighs. "That's because I mean to win."

She sucked in her breath. "You're playing dirty."

He wasn't about to deny that. "Like I said, I mean to win."

There had to be ground rules, otherwise she was just

going to get pulled into the vortex and disappear without a trace. "I won't give up my career."

He began tracing the outline of her face with his lips. "No one's asking you to."

"And I'll be gone almost all the time..." He reached her neck. "Well, maybe a lot...." His hands were slowly massaging her, sending arrows of desire all through her. "...once in a while."

"We'll work it out," he promised, lightly brushing his lips against hers. "We'll work out everything."

He'd won, lock, stock and barrel. And he was right, she wasn't her mother and he wasn't her father. He was far too selfless to be compared to the shadow of the man from her childhood. They could make this work. They *would* make this work.

Hands on his shoulders, she smiled up into his face. "You do drive a hard bargain."

He had his victory and silently made her a vow that she would never regret saying yes. "Like I keep saying, I mean to win."

She brought her body closer to his. So close she could feel the sizzle pass from him to her. "Have you got a closing argument?"

"No." Tugging her sweater up over her head, he tossed it aside and took her back into his arms. "But I have a beginning one."

And it was a doozy.

Epilogue

Jimmy heard a knock on the door behind him. "Come in." Glancing up at his patient, he could tell by the admiring look in the man's eyes exactly who had entered. Only one person would have breezed into his office as if she had an absolute right to be here.

"Hello, April," he said without turning around.

April stopped dead in the doorway. "How did you know it was me?"

"A husband develops this sixth sense about his wife's whereabouts," he told her sagely as he turned around, his serious expression not giving him away.

April laughed. Yeah, right. "We've been married less than two months." Two glorious, lovemaking-filled months that had seen her reassess her priorities. So much so that she hadn't even given leaving Hades as much as a single thought.

"I'm a fast learner." He saw the magazine she was clutching in her hand. So that was it. Everything came together. Taking a bottle out of the large medicine cabinet, he handed it to his patient, Dimitri Mac-Gregor. "Take two of these every time you feel the pain coming on, and stay away from fried foods."

"Right." Dimitri laughed, passing April as he went to the door. He nodded at her just before he pocketed the bottle and left the room.

Jimmy put out his hand. "Well, let's see it."

"See what?" April asked innocently, coyly holding the magazine behind her back. "Maybe I just came to see my husband."

"You came to preen and we both know it." He beckoned to her. "C'mon, let's have a look and see if they did you justice."

Unable to contain her exuberance any longer, April flipped open the magazine, a well-respected vacation periodical, and turned to the pages that held the photographs she'd worked so hard to get just right. "They did. Look." She held them up for his inspection.

He took the magazine from her, pride swelling in his chest as he looked at the pages. Splashed across a twelve-page section were photographs April had taken of both Hades and the surrounding area. They captured the terrain with an intimate familiarity that reflected a deep-seated affection.

No doubt about it, she was good. He slipped his arm around her shoulders, pulling her to him. "Did your grandmother see this?"

Making herself comfortable in the space created by the crook of his arm, she grinned at him. She would be eternally grateful to him for what he did for Gran. Thanks to him, she'd been strong enough to have her by-pass surgery and was behaving like a teenager again. "She's the postmistress, what do you think?"

"I think half of Alaska has just been put on alert to buy this month's issue of *The Happy Wanderer*." Jimmy looked down at the last page, where credit for the photographs was given. *April Yearling-Quintano*. It was a mouthful. And she was a handful, one he knew he would never tire of handling. "Not bad for a woman who can't stand the place."

A smile tugged at her mouth. "Oh, it has some redeeming qualities," April murmured, looking up at him, her light tone belying the excitement and happiness she felt.

But she didn't fool Jimmy. In tune to her every thought, he knew exactly what she was feeling. Like a woman who had finally, truly come home.

Leaning over, he kissed her.

Bemused, she ran the tip of her tongue over her lips. "What was that for?"

"A down payment for later," he promised her in a whisper that had her blood stirring.

She could hardly wait for later to come.

* * * * *

Look for Marie Ferrarella's next story,
"The Baby in the Cabbage Patch,"
available in MATERNITY LEAVE 2001,
on sale in July 2001,
only from Silhouette Books.

If you enjoyed what you just read,
then we've got an offer you can't resist!

Take 2 bestselling
love stories FREE!
Plus get a FREE surprise gift!

Clip this page and mail it to Silhouette Reader Service™

IN U.S.A.	IN CANADA
3010 Walden Ave.	P.O. Box 609
P.O. Box 1867	Fort Erie, Ontario
Buffalo, N.Y. 14240-1867	L2A 5X3

YES! Please send me 2 free Silhouette Special Edition® novels and my free surprise gift. Then send me 6 brand-new novels every month, which I will receive months before they're available in stores. In the U.S.A., bill me at the bargain price of $3.80 plus 25¢ delivery per book and applicable sales tax, if any*. In Canada, bill me at the bargain price of $4.21 plus 25¢ delivery per book and applicable taxes**. That's the complete price and a savings of at least 10% off the cover prices—what a great deal! I understand that accepting the 2 free books and gift places me under no obligation ever to buy any books. I can always return a shipment and cancel at any time. Even if I never buy another book from Silhouette, the 2 free books and gift are mine to keep forever. So why not take us up on our invitation. You'll be glad you did!

235 SEN C224
335 SEN C225

Name	(PLEASE PRINT)	
Address	Apt.#	
City	State/Prov.	Zip/Postal Code

* Terms and prices subject to change without notice. Sales tax applicable in N.Y.
** Canadian residents will be charged applicable provincial taxes and GST.
   All orders subject to approval. Offer limited to one per household.
   ® are registered trademarks of Harlequin Enterprises Limited.

Feel like a star with Silhouette.

We will fly you and a guest to New York City for an exciting weekend stay at a glamorous 5-star hotel. Experience a refreshing day at one of New York's trendiest spas and have your photo taken by a professional. Plus, receive $1,000 U.S. spending money!

Flowers...long walks...dinner for two... how does Silhouette Books make romance come alive for you?

Send us a script, with 500 words or less, along with visuals (only drawings, magazine cutouts or photographs or combination thereof). Show us how Silhouette Makes Your Love Come Alive. Be creative and have fun. No purchase necessary. All entries must be clearly marked with your name, address and telephone number. All entries will become property of Silhouette and are not returnable. **Contest closes September 28, 2001.**

Please send your entry to: **Silhouette Makes You a Star!**

In U.S.A.
P.O. Box 9069
Buffalo, NY, 14269-9069

In Canada
P.O. Box 637
Fort Erie, ON, L2A 5X3

Look for contest details on the next page, by visiting www.eHarlequin.com or request a copy by sending a self-addressed envelope to the applicable address above. Contest open to Canadian and U.S. residents who are 18 or over. Void where prohibited.

Silhouette®
Where love comes alive™

Our lucky winner's photo will appear in a Silhouette ad. Join the fun!

HARLEQUIN "SILHOUETTE MAKES YOU A STAR!" CONTEST 1308
OFFICIAL RULES
NO PURCHASE NECESSARY TO ENTER

1. To enter, follow directions published in the offer to which you are responding. Contest begins June 1, 2001, and ends on September 28, 2001. Entries must be postmarked by September 28, 2001, and received by October 5, 2001. Enter by hand-printing (or typing) on an 8 ½" x 11" piece of paper your name, address (including zip code), contest number/name and attaching a script containing 500 words or less, along with drawings, photographs or magazine cutouts, or combinations thereof (i.e., collage) on no larger than 9" x 12" piece of paper, describing how the Silhouette books make romance come alive for you. Mail via first-class mail to: Harlequin "Silhouette Makes You a Star!" Contest 1308, (in the U.S.) P.O. Box 9069, Buffalo, NY 14269-9069, (in Canada) P.O. Box 637, Fort Erie, Ontario, Canada L2A 5X3. Limit one entry per person, household or organization.

2. Contests will be judged by a panel of members of the Harlequin editorial, marketing and public relations staff. Fifty percent of criteria will be judged against script and fifty percent will be judged against drawing, photographs and/or magazine cutouts. Judging criteria will be based on the following:

    - Sincerity—25%
    - Originality and Creativity—50%
    - Emotionally Compelling—25%

   In the event of a tie, duplicate prizes will be awarded. Decisions of the judges are final.

3. All entries become the property of Torstar Corp. and may be used for future promotional purposes. Entries will not be returned. No responsibility is assumed for lost, late, illegible, incomplete, inaccurate, nondelivered or misdirected mail.

4. Contest open only to residents of the U.S. (except Puerto Rico) and Canada who are 18 years of age or older, and is void wherever prohibited by law; all applicable laws and regulations apply. Any litigation within the Province of Quebec respecting the conduct or organization of a publicity contest may be submitted to the Régie des alcools, des courses et des jeux for a ruling. Any litigation respecting the awarding of a prize may be submitted to the Régie des alcools, des courses et des jeux only for the purpose of helping the parties reach a settlement. Employees and immediate family members of Torstar Corp. and D. L. Blair, Inc., their affiliates, subsidiaries and all other agencies, entities and persons connected with the use, marketing or conduct of this contest are not eligible to enter. Taxes on prizes are the sole responsibility of the winner. Acceptance of any prize offered constitutes permission to use winner's name, photograph or other likeness for the purposes of advertising, trade and promotion on behalf of Torstar Corp., its affiliates and subsidiaries without further compensation to the winner, unless prohibited by law.

5. Winner will be determined no later than November 30, 2001, and will be notified by mail. Winner will be required to sign and return an Affidavit of Eligibility/Release of Liability/Publicity Release form within 15 days after winner notification. Noncompliance within that time period may result in disqualification and an alternative winner may be selected. All travelers must execute a Release of Liability prior to ticketing and must possess required travel documents (e.g., passport, photo ID) where applicable. Trip must be booked by December 31, 2001, and completed within one year of notification. No substitution of prize permitted by winner. Torstar Corp. and D. L. Blair, Inc., their parents, affiliates and subsidiaries are not responsible for errors in printing of contest, entries and/or game pieces. In the event of printing or other errors that may result in unintended prize values or duplication of prizes, all affected game pieces or entries shall be null and void. **Purchase or acceptance of a product offer does not improve your chances of winning.**

6. Prizes: (1) Grand Prize—A 2-night/3-day trip for two (2) to New York City, including round-trip coach air transportation nearest winner's home and hotel accommodations (double occupancy) at The Plaza Hotel, a glamorous afternoon makeover at a trendy New York spa, $1,000 in U.S. spending money and an opportunity to have a professional photo taken and appear in a Silhouette advertisement (approximate retail value: $7,000). (10) Ten Runner-Up Prizes of gift packages (retail value $50 ea.). Prizes consist of only those items listed as part of the prize. Limit one prize per person. Prize is valued in U.S. currency.

7. For the name of the winner (available after December 31, 2001) send a self-addressed, stamped envelope to: Harlequin "Silhouette Makes You a Star!" Contest 1197 Winners, P.O. Box 4200 Blair, NE 68009-4200 or you may access the www.eHarlequin.com Web site through February 28, 2002.

Contest sponsored by Torstar Corp., P.O Box 9042, Buffalo, NY 14269-9042.

Available in August from

JOAN ELLIOTT PICKART

A brand-new, longer-length book
in the bestselling series,

The Baby Bet

*Party
of Three*

He was a hard-boiled cop with a child in his care.
She was a woman in need of his protective embrace.
Together they were a family in the making....

*Available at your favorite retail outlet.
Only from Silhouette Books*

Silhouette®
Where love comes alive™

Bestselling author

LISA JACKSON

brings you more of the powerful and loyal
McCafferty family.

Coming in July 2001 from

SPECIAL EDITION™

The McCaffertys: Matt

Matt McCafferty never met a woman who didn't succumb
to the McCafferty charm. But beautiful Kelly Dillinger was
proving indifferent to his attractions. Although they didn't
get along, her all-business attitude pricked
his ego…and fired his blood. The
more that she resisted, the more
determined he became to break
down her defenses.…

And don't miss
Slade McCafferty's
story coming to
Silhouette Special Edition
in early 2002 .

THE McCAFFERTYS:
A mystery baby leads three brothers to
love under the wide Montana sky.

Available at your favorite retail outlet.

Silhouette®
Where love comes alive™

Visit Silhouette at www.eHarlequin.com   SSEMCC